MAIMED

Joanna Coles was driving her children to school, as she did every morning of term time. On this particular dreary December day, however, a decision was being made about her, a decision of which she knew nothing. Soon after Christmas, Joanna Coles would be a name known to millions. Her photograph would appear on the television and in every newspaper in the land. Unfortunately, Joanna would know nothing of her tragic fame . . .

LYN JOLLEY

◆

MAIMED

Complete and Unabridged

LINFORD
Leicester

First published in Great Britain

First Linford Edition
published 2008

British Library CIP Data

Jolley, Lyn
    Maimed.—Large print ed.—
Linford mystery library
    1. Suspense fiction
    2. Large type books
    I. Title
    823.9'2 [F]

    ISBN 978–1–84782–259–8

Published by
F. A. Thorpe (Publishing)
Anstey, Leicestershire

Set by Words & Graphics Ltd.
Anstey, Leicestershire
Printed and bound in Great Britain by
T. J. International Ltd., Padstow, Cornwall

This book is printed on acid-free paper

PROLOGUE

Joanna Coles was driving her children to school, as she did every morning of term time. On this particular dreary December day, however, a decision was being made about her, a decision of which she knew nothing.

Soon after Christmas, Joanna Coles would be a name known to millions. Her photograph would appear on the television and in every newspaper in the land. Unfortunately, Joanna would know nothing of her tragic fame.

'Right, Miss Sammy Coles, out you get. Have you got your lunch box?'

Joanna took her daughter's gloved hand and guided her to the gates of St. Steven's Infant School. Five year old Samantha deposited a loud kiss on her mother's cheek and ran eagerly into the playground, where she greeted her numerous friends with squeals of delight and the spontaneous hugs of affection which subside as childhood recedes and inhibitions take hold.

The teacher on playground duty raised a reassuring hand to Joanna, who rushed back to her car knowing that the younger of her offspring was safely delivered.

'Now then, young Ben,' Joanna enthused, 'off we go again. Next stop — Darley Hill.'

Nine year old Benjamin Coles grunted a muffled acknowledgement of his mother's words. He dribbled down his navy coat and his head jerked involuntarily in every direction that his ungovernable muscles would allow.

Joanna's new estate car halted sedately on the drive of Darley Hill Special School.

'Here we are then, darling,' she chirped, retrieving Ben's folded wheelchair from the back of the car. 'Now, when I come to collect you, I want Mrs. Ballard to tell me that you've tried really hard at school today.'

Ben was not listening. His attention was directed at his mother's efficient hands, as she made his wheelchair ready

2

for use. He tried to ease himself from the car, while Joanna slid her arms around his frail form and lifted him with optimum gentleness into his chair. A tissue was quickly produced and Ben's chin wiped dry. Then, with hurried steps, Joanna pushed her son to the door of the school.

Darley Hill Special School was one of the finest in the country. It offered the most up-to-date facilities and resources needed for the education of handicapped children such as Ben. Joanna and Stuart, her husband, had moved to Darley New Town so that Ben could take up the place offered to him by such a prestigious school, and, at the same time, enjoy as normal a home life as possible. They could not bear the thought of their son living in an institution.

The move had turned out to be no hardship for the caring young couple. They loved the New Forest which edged their home, and took Samantha and Ben for picnics every weekend in the warm weather. Stuart's bank had given him, not only a transfer, but also promotion to the position of manager of the Darley branch, and Joanna had taken a job as secretary at the local grammar school, the hours fitting in well with her own children's schooling. The most pleasing outcome of their exodus from London, however, was that their children had settled happily in their schools, and Ben appeared to be making some progress, albeit very slow and inconsistent.

Having given her son over to his physiotherapist, always the first session of his school day, Joanna drove to work.

Once in the grammar school car park, she checked her face and hair in the driving mirror. She need not have bothered; her well-groomed appearance rarely needed refurbishment. Her thick, black hair fell in a short bob and always looked as though it had just been shampooed, while her tastefully applied makeup accentuated her brown, compassionate eyes and her expressive lips. Joanna was a little over five feet tall and very slim. She moved as though a surfeit of energy within her could not be contained. It was as if each and every

4

action afforded her exhilaration. Joanna was quite lovely.

Two secretaries manned the office of the Darley New Town Grammar School, Jean Barnett being Joanna's senior and, at the same time, her best friend. Since taking up her duties at the school, Joanna had found Jean to be a kindred spirit, and the two women passed their working days in mutual affability.

Often Jean, and her husband Peter, would spend an evening with Joanna and Stuart, always at the home of the latter couple because of Ben. Joanna wished she could feel certain that Jean and Peter's visits were not born from pity and endured rather than enjoyed, but she could not; their friendship was still too young.

There was no way that Ben could be left while his parents went out, however. His very special needs made it difficult for the average baby-sitter to cope, and Joanna and Stuart found it easier to entertain in their own home, rather than to spend the evening worrying about what could be going wrong in their absence.

They also feared that Ben would be embarrassed by the attentions of someone other than the two of them or the carers at his school. He was unable to control his bladder and bowels properly, and his parents knew that he was sensitive about this; he did not even like his sister in the room when he was changed or toileted, though the cheerful and gregarious Samantha took such matters in her stride. She loved her brother with the unquestioning devotion which is unique to the early years of childhood. Whenever possible, she helped Joanna and Stuart to look after Ben, and only showed jealousy at the amount of attention which he demanded on the rarest of occasions.

At quarter past three every afternoon, Joanna left work and collected, first Samantha, and then Ben from school. She loved this part of the day. Once at home, Samantha would play with her brother or look at picture books with him, while Joanna prepared the meal and tidied the house. When Stuart came in from the bank, her world was as perfect as her circumstances would allow it to be.

The hours until their bedtime were for the children, and only after they were asleep could Joanna and Stuart relax and talk. Even then, their evenings were often disturbed, as Ben frequently needed attention at night, attention which was always given unselfishly by both his parents.

Life was busy for Joanna Coles, but she needed to be fully occupied. Time on her hands only left her wondering why.

Stuart had long since accepted Ben's condition, but Joanna had not. Though, ostensibly she was in control of her feelings and coping marvellously with her son's chronic disabilities, she could find no answer, no reason why Ben should be so abnormal — so imperfect.

She no longer believed in God, or at least, she had decided long ago that if there were such a being, the fact that he allowed so many cruel things to happen in his world, and to the people he is supposed to love, made him unworthy of the praise and adoration given freely by so many.

Joanna hoped that one day she would

come to terms with her son's sad plight, or at least gain some understanding of why Ben had been so mercilessly singled out.

How she wished that those dreams would stop: dreams of a healthy boy with Ben's face running to greet her, dreams which teased her with sheer delight until her waking. Then, with the onslaught of stark reality, came a heaviness which dragged her heart down into a hideously familiar abyss. At such moments, Joanna knew absolute despair — a despair that the world must never witness — would never witness.

It was not only her dreams which made the night a time of raw anguish for Joanna. Often she would lie awake in the hostile darkness and just think of Ben — of his future — his past . . . his birth.

* * *

'That's right, Joanna, push — come on — push — make the most of it. Wipe your wife's forehead, will you, Mr. Coles. I can

8

see the head, Joanna — you're nearly there!'

'I just want to go to sleep.'

'I know, but you wait till you see your baby, you'll be wide awake then. Come on — work hard — push. That's it — nearly there — yes good — bit more — yes! It's a boy! You've got a son, Joanna . . . I'm just going to clear his tubes.'

'He isn't crying — why isn't he crying? Can I see him?'

'Sister is going to clear his airways, Mrs. Coles. He's a bit choked up. Don't worry. It often happens.'

Spasms of troubled consciousness followed, amid hours of drugged slumber, until:

'Doctor, what's wrong? Let me see my baby — where is he?'

'He's in need of special care, Mrs. Coles. I'm afraid there are problems . . . quite serious problems.'

★   ★   ★

Then the tears always came, and after the tears, an uneasy sleep.

9

Her hope that some acceptance of her son's condition would be hers in time was a futile one, because Joanna did not have much time. The final few days of her life were passing quickly and irretrievably by.

'Salt, mustard, vinegar, pepper, salt, mustard, vinegar, pepper . . . ' The man who was to terminate Joanna Coles's existence watched as her daughter tried, with limited success, to master the intricate art of skipping. Little Samantha chanted monotonously as she made ungainly attempts to control the wayward rope. Joanna made Ben comfortable in the back of her car and then bundled a protesting Samantha in too.

The car had soon gone round the corner, but the little girl's chanting remained in the mind of the hidden observer, forcing him to remember.

★　★　★

His tiny hands gripped the railings of a school playground. He could feel again the coldness of the iron bars on his soft cheeks as he stared in at the children.

Little girls were skipping and chanting — just like Samantha Coles. Boys were kicking a football and shouting, more to hear the loudness of their own voices than to convey a message to their fellow players. Then:

'Miss Thomson! Miss Thomson — James has fallen over! He's cut his knee open — it's bleeding, Miss Thomson!'

'All right — don't worry, James, we'll soon have a plaster on it. Come with me.'

The unruffled teacher took a tearful and bloody James into the school building for attention. Football resumed.

He had been watching then too. The little boy with his face against the bars had never been one of the children in the playground — he had always looked on.

★　★　★

A car passed by him, noisily throwing up stones from the lane and causing the watcher to return to the present.

It was different now, he watched because he wanted to. A few weeks ago, it had been necessary for him to learn

11

Joanna's daily routine, so that he could decide where and when she would die — he already knew how. Now that his plans were complete, however, the stalking of his victim was a pleasure which he savoured, rather than a necessity. The fact that he was so often there, with her, yet without her knowledge, gave him great satisfaction.

On this particular morning, the last of the school term before the Christmas holidays, he had watched the children and Joanna leave from a quiet, tree-lined lane near their home. Stuart had left for work much earlier.

The prospective murderer had no real interest in Joanna's husband, only in the hours he did not spend with her . . . the hours she was alone.

It was time to leave his hide. He would not go to the woods near the grammar school car park this morning, so that he could watch her arriving at her office, there was no need . . . he would be seeing Joanna again, later that day.

★ ★ ★

Red and gold decorations hung from the ceiling of the Darley Hill Special School dining room, while huge collections of balloons adorned each corner, like bunches of some weird and inedible fruit. The dining tables edged the room, covered with red crêpe paper and a profusion of tempting party foods to accommodate any taste. While, beside the large, double doors a sweet-smelling Christmas tree dominated the proceedings with its glittering grandeur.

Joanna had arranged with Jean that she should leave work early on the last afternoon of term, in order to attend the Christmas party at Ben's school. Now, as she held her son's hand and sang 'Jingle Bells' with the rest of the parents, and those children who could make some attempt to join in, she wished that she were somewhere else — anywhere else. Such occasions seemed to Joanna, to be a pitiful attempt to mimic normality. She was certain that something must be lacking in her own personality, otherwise, why would a party evoke such an attitude? Yet, looking around the room, it was as though these children were being patronized — kindly so — but, nevertheless, patronized. It was as if the adults present were saying, 'this is how able-bodied people enjoy themselves, children — this is the way you must have fun.' These dear children were not like the rest of us and never could be; surely such indoctrination into the ways of those who are 'normal' must smother their own needs and pleasures. Joanna wished that her son could have more freedom to be himself, and less education in the art of being like the rest of humanity.

Ben had been captured, though. On the day of his birth, the day of his separation from Joanna's body, when his own independent life should have begun, he had been captured, and his was a life-long sentence, without a trial. There could be no freedom for Ben.

'Away in a Manger' was now in full swing. Joanna's murderer was singing too; he had always loved Christmas carols.

After a raucous rendition of 'We Three Kings', there was a fanfare, performed by one of the fathers who could almost play

14

the cornet. A weak parental cheer went up when Father Christmas entered the room with a large, bulging sack in tow. Most of the children looked on in dismay, except for little Jasmine Yacksley, who went into fits of hysterical screaming, and had to be wheeled out of the room by her embarrassed mother.

Alex Dunbar, a wealthy woman in the neighbourhood who raised funds for the school in all kinds of ways, had persuaded her younger son, Toby, to play the part of Santa Claus. He was only twenty-three, but he gave both presents and hugs like a veteran.

Chaos reigned. New drums were beaten, squeaks and squeals came from various cuddly toys and the odd dispute broke out among the children over the finer points of the laws concerning possession.

Joanna wound up a mechanical spotty dog which had been Ben's surprise. She placed it in front of his wheelchair and it paraded along the floor for him. Ben frowned — totally fascinated. Joanna smiled with her eyes, but her heart cried.

Guy Dunbar, Alex's elder son, picked up the flagging dog in passing, and rewound it for Ben, then he went off to help his brother who was still reaching to the bottom of the sack for the final few presents.

Joanna thought what unselfish young men the Dunbars must be, giving up their time to help on such occasions as this, which would find most single males running away at high speed.

In fact, Guy Dunbar was a regular visitor to the school. His father owned a stud farm and stables near Darley New Town, and Guy and his mother frequently brought very docile horses to the school. Guy would watch as Alex gave the children pony rides around the paddock.

It was time for food. The children were wheeled or carried to the tables, where parents and staff attempted to ensure that everyone had a fair share.

Next to Ben and Joanna were Michael Gilchrist and his son, Giles. Joanna had always felt very sorry for Michael because his wife had left him soon after Giles's birth. On this particular afternoon, however, the lone father seemed to be nudging himself far more closely against her than was necessary. She tried to ignore this, but when his hand slid under the crêpe tablecloth and onto her knee, she glared at him and moved around to the other side of Ben's chair.

When the messy business of feeding Ben was over, Joanna began, along with several other mothers, to clear away the debris of the meal; her killer watched contentedly. As she chatted cheerfully to children and parents alike, he mused, with smug satisfaction, on how little she really knew.

There she was, capability and charm emanating from her, like mischief from a puppy. She appeared so confident and so very perfect; he longed to destroy her world . . . or rather, her. He was not totally free from doubt, however. To deprive humanity of someone so lovely was, in one way, a sad task, but a task that must be carried out.

Then, Joanna passed closely by him, so closely that he wanted to stretch out his hand and touch her clear, olive skin. He felt as though cold water was running from his neck to the base of his spine. Her perfume drifted around him, delicate and fresh. It soothed him. He felt powerful — in control of life and death — Joanna's life and death.

Small coats were buttoned up, hats and gloves were awkwardly manoeuvred on to complaining offspring; the party was over.

Victim and murderer smiled at each other and said goodbye.

Calls of, 'Merry Christmas!' hovered and collided on the cool air, as car doors slammed and engines started reluctantly.

It was dusk when Joanna and Ben drove away from Darley Hill School.

Her killer would allow her to have Christmas with her family . . . yes, predator and prey would meet early in the new year . . . for the very last time.

1

'Oh, Guy, that's beautiful! Thank you, darling.' Alex Dunbar took a large, round brooch from its presentation box. 'Rubies too — my favourite!' she enthused, pinning it to her lapel.

Christmas morning in the Dunbar household was a traditional affair. Alex, Phillip and their two sons sat by the Christmas tree in their luxurious drawing room opening their presents.

'Oh hell!' Toby exclaimed. 'Aunt Edith's bought me yet another set of cufflinks!'

'That means I'll have some too,' Guy replied sympathetically. 'When will she realize that we don't wear them?'

'Perhaps you will when you're older,' Alex scolded, 'you mustn't be ungrateful.'

Toby and Guy grinned at each other, and then continued to tear the obligatory gaudy paper from their gifts.

By the time the presents had all been

unwrapped and hugs of gratitude distributed liberally between members of the Dunbar family, the Persian rug in front of the imposing marble fireplace was ankle deep in shredded paper, labels and shiny bows.

'Before we get this lot cleared up,' Phillip announced, 'there's one more present which couldn't be fitted under the Christmas tree. Come on, Toby — give me a hand.'

Father and younger son left the room excitedly. Alex smiled knowingly at Guy, whose bewilderment was obvious, and touched his hand.

After a few minutes, Phillip and Toby returned, carefully wheeling a display stand on which stood an enormous fish tank tied with a huge, golden ribbon.

'We thought it would be an entertaining hobby for you, darling,' his mother whispered.

Guy was indeed surprised, or perhaps shocked. He approached the tank as though it were housing a killer whale. Slowly he undid the ostentatious bow so that he could see the contents clearly.

'They're rare tropical fish,' his father explained. 'You can breed them and add to your collection — more tanks and so on.'

'It — it's great!' Guy said, touching the cool glass with what appeared to be fondness. 'I don't know what to say . . . thank you!'

He turned and hugged his mother, kissing her cheek warmly.

'I've got you this to go with it,' Toby enthused, passing a large, glossy reference book to his brother. 'It tells you everything you need to know about tropical fish and how to breed them.'

'Thanks, Toby!' Guy touched his brother's shoulder. 'And you too, Dad, it's a fantastic present!'

'We'd better get all this paraphernalia into your rooms, Guy,' Phillip suggested. 'We've had the tank plugged in all night in the breakfast room — we mustn't let the temperature drop.'

The bulky gift was duly transported into Guy's sitting room, where it stood defiantly against the wall.

'I'll go and get their food,' Toby

volunteered, 'it's hidden in the kitchen.'

'Quite beautiful, aren't they?' Alex said wistfully, as she looked in at the brightly coloured fish.

'Mm — lovely,' Guy agreed, browsing through his book.

'Well, I'll leave you to sort out their feeding, darling. Don't be too long — Aunt Kate will be here soon for lunch.'

Toby returned, dumped the fish-food at Guy's feet and departed hastily to become acquainted with his new computer.

Guy was alone with his gift.

He stood, tall and slim, in front of the fish tank, staring at the small, aquatic prisoners. His handsome face was expressionless as his wide, grey eyes followed the monotonous movements of these delicate creatures.

Suddenly Guy caught a glimpse of his reflection in the side of the tank, and its inhabitants were momentarily displaced from his thoughts by vanity.

He turned his head from side to side to inspect both profiles, as he did in the mirror quite frequently. It was truly amazing, he pondered, that some people considered himself and Toby to be so similar in appearance that they believed them to be twins. Certainly, his brother was a good-looking young man, but Toby did not have the high cheekbones and strong jaw-line that made his own face so striking. They both had their mother's thick, brown hair and gun-metal eyes, but apart from that, Guy considered the resemblance between he and his brother to be much overstated.

He ran his slender fingers along the top of the tank . . . yes, just as he thought, the corners had been rounded — no sharp edges.

Guy wondered if the fish were aware of his presence. His mother was right — they were beautiful. Some — he had no idea of their correct name — were the most vivid turquoise. It was as though their colour revealed an insistence, albeit a silent one, that they must be noticed. Their fellow tank-dwellers were mostly pearly silver, but a few shone in the colour of coral — deep and sensuous. Round and round they went . . . round and round in hopeless tedium, just like those ghastly, ridiculous trains. It had been a time for acting then too — that awful Christmas ten years ago.

★　★　★

'Your special present is hidden up in one of the attic rooms,' Alex said, excitedly guiding her elder son up to the top of the vast house.

Phillip and Toby followed, both giggling. Guy himself was alive with exquisite anticipation on this, his fifteenth Christmas morning. His mother's hand gripped the door handle, and his heart seemed to falter in his chest, while his breath hung, trapped in his throat. Surely this year he would have the golden retriever puppy he had always longed for — yes, it must be that — it would be waiting for him behind the attic room door — plump and soft and playful. He strained to hear its whimpers, but perhaps it was asleep in a blanket-lined basket.

As his mother pushed open the door, revealing a huge electric train set, Guy struggled to gulp back a tear. Toby hugged his brother, convinced, like his parents, that it was joy which moistened Guy's clear, young eyes. It was, however, a deep and indescribable disappointment.

'Have a look then, son,' Phillip urged, delighted with the gift which had been his idea. 'There are villages — see — and towns . . . and your controls are over here — come and have a go!'

Guy walked to where his father stood pointing to the buttons which drove the boring trains around the track.

'It's great, Dad!' he whispered, his mind fierce with profound hatred for his family.

'Look, you can work the signals with this one,' Phillip continued.

'It is Guy's, darling,' Alex reminded her husband.

'Yes, Dad,' Toby put in, 'let Guy do it — it's his present!'

'I'm only showing him,' Phillip protested, 'someone's got to show him how to work it.'

Guy looked at his parents and Toby. Why could he not scream at them that he hated the trains? Why could he not tell them that he loathed them for giving him such a stupid present? Why could he not let all that anger out, instead of holding it inside himself like a dormant volcano waiting to spew the boiling, deadly contents of its gut out at the unsuspecting world?

Guy smiled broadly.

'It's a fantastic present,' he said.

He could not hurt them, because, with the same heart and mind which loathed them, he loved his parents and Toby dearly.

'Right, now it's your turn for a special present, Toby,' Alex exclaimed. 'Everyone downstairs!'

'You can come back to your trains in a minute, Guy,' Phillip reassured, totally ignorant of the fact that the last place Guy wanted to be was up in that attic with those hateful trains.

Toby ran on ahead down the final flight of stairs, which led from the attic rooms to the spacious main hallway of Dunbar House.

'Where is it?' he demanded, hopping

26

about from foot to foot and waving his arms in the air. 'Which room?'

'Calm down, Toby,' his mother urged.

'Follow me!' Phillip instructed, unable to conceal his own joy, and walking rapidly towards the back door.

Toby needed no second bidding.

The sharp winter air nipped at the warm faces of the Dunbars as they crossed the courtyard to one of the stables.

Guy knew now what his brother's present was. His envy was acute and engulfed him like a blanket full of needles.

The stable door opened and Toby approached the young Arab stallion, which was his gift, with genuine tears of delight running down his cheeks.

'He's a year old,' his father explained, stroking the horse's neck with the confidence which comes from years of working with such splendid animals.

'You're lucky that I've done such a lot of business with the sheik this year; he let me buy this chap at a knock down price, and your mother and I knew how much you wanted your own horse. We could have simply given you one from our own stables, of course, but that wouldn't have seemed right somehow. Anyway, an Arab is so special.'

'I don't know what to say!' Toby blubbed. 'He's the most wonderful . . . '

'Don't say anything,' Phillip murmured, patting Toby's back, 'just saddle him up and go for a ride . . . he's got an excellent temperament.'

'Come on, Guy — stand well back.' Alex guided her elder son away from the stable door. 'Your father says he's gentle, but I've seen so many of them kick out when they're saddled up. You mustn't take any risks, darling.'

Later that morning, while Christmas dinner was being prepared, Guy watched from the attic room window as Toby rode his horse through to the paddocks. He saw him trot and then gallop across the grounds of Dunbar House, until horse and rider looked like small mechanical toys against a painted, rural backdrop. Such freedom!

Guy turned to the trains, sobbing with

utter misery. He pressed the buttons which sent the miniature rolling-stock around its expensive but unreal world. Round it went — round and round — all pretence — and all imprisoned in the attic of Dunbar House and the mind of Guy Dunbar.

He should have known better than to hope for a puppy; Guy rebuked himself — a child's unsuccessful attempt to rationalize his plight and come to terms with an unfair world. His mother would never let him have an animal which might scratch or dig its teeth into his hands — albeit in play. And as for a horse, which might kick or bite or throw him — no such risks must be taken. It was all for his own good . . . for his protection.

Guy curled up in the corner of the room and sobbed until his head and throat ached. He had never before known such absolute desolation.

★   ★   ★

Now, the pain was not in his head and throat, but his heart was as leaden as it

29

had been ten years ago, and Guy suddenly realized that his hands were hurting. He had been clutching his new book so tightly that the joints in his fingers had become very painful. He tossed the book aside, not caring where it fell. These bitter memories had caused his heart to pummel against his breast-bone, and the intense anger, an old acquaintance, had forced his jaws to set tightly against each other.

Guy smiled down at the fish, shook his head slowly and then walked to the other side of the room and picked up a heavy, brass paperweight. He held it high in the air and then hurled it, with all his savage strength, at the fish tank. The noise was deafening as the glass appeared to explode outwards into the room, and water gushed, like Lilliputian falls, onto the hitherto immaculate carpet, carrying the helpless little fish with it. Guy rushed towards the debris and grabbed up the brass paperweight from the squelching carpet, returning it to its usual home just as the door of his sitting room was thrust open.

'Guy — darling!' His mother, panicking, rushed to his side. 'Are you hurt, Guy? Are you cut or anything?' she pleaded.

'No,' he replied, feigning shock to Oscar-winning standards, 'no, I'm all right — don't worry.'

'What the hell happened?' Phillip demanded, as he and Toby entered.

'The tank exploded,' Guy explained, a false bewilderment concealing his guilt.

'But it can't have done!' Phillip argued.

'Don't be so ridiculous, Phillip!' Alex snapped. 'There's your proof!' She pointed at the mess. 'It's a miracle that Guy wasn't cut — when I think of what might have happened.'

Alex held on to her son's arm, as though needing proof of his safety, a proof which she could only find in physical contact with him.

Guy was unaware of his family's concern at this moment. He was mesmerized by the sight of the tiny fish. A few were still flapping in pitiful and futile panic, desperate for the life-giving water, which now soaked deeper into the thick

31

carpet pile that was their death-bed.

'Poor little buggers,' Toby whispered.

'Yes, just get it all cleared up will you, Toby,' Alex said brusquely, leading Guy into his bedroom. 'And nothing like that must ever be brought into this house again!'

Phillip, having unplugged the tank, looked on, bemused by the whole affair, as Toby began to do his mother's bidding.

'You must lie down for a while,' Alex insisted, plumping up the pillows on Guy's bed.

'I told you, Mother, I'm perfectly all right,' Guy answered with some agitation, 'please don't fuss.'

'It's a shock for you, Guy. Now, just lie here and rest until the lunch is ready — to please me.'

'O.K. If I must,' Guy sighed in acquiescence.

'Yes — you must.'

Alex turned to leave the room.

'I'm sorry, Mother.' Guy murmured.

'Sorry, darling? What for?'

'I'm sorry that your lovely present went wrong.'

'The only thing that matters is that you weren't hurt, Guy — to hell with the present!'

Alex left her son alone to rest.

Guy closed his eyes and smiled broadly, a menacing satisfaction spreading across his classical features. After only a few seconds peace, however, that persistent outrage returned to control his mind again.

How could they have bought him that? Guy reminded himself silently and swiftly that he should know better than to be mystified by the actions of his loving relatives after all these years. They had conspired to give him the fish tank, in all innocence, because they had truly believed that he would enjoy the gift. Their ignorance of the truth was not their fault; they did not see the world as he did. How could they? He should not feel such fury towards them . . . but he did.

Guy pictured Toby, clearing up the glass and fish corpses in the next room. Poor old Toby, their mother would not be frantic if he should cut himself. Guy loved his younger brother very much. His envy of Toby was constant and immense, because Toby was normal and strong and not a haemophiliac, but then Guy knew envy very well; it had always been his closest companion. Toby could not be blamed for his healthy blood, however, any more than he could be blamed for having haemophilia — only one person was responsible for that.

Guy felt strangely reassured when he thought about his relationship with his brother. They had been good friends since early childhood — as close as Guy's condition would allow. Of course, Toby could help his father with the running of the stud farm, with the practical things. He had always worked in the stables and he loved to ride, whereas Guy had never been able to, in case he should be thrown or kicked by a fractious animal.

Guy pondered again, as if he were compelled to punish himself, on the hundreds of times he had watched from his well-padded rooms as Toby had thundered past on horseback, galloping in a euphoric daze, his hair blown straight by the wind and the sheer enjoyment of speed on his face.

Guy had always realized that Toby's life should not be restricted because of his haemophilia, of course not. He would never allow that to happen, but he was certain that he could have had more freedom in his own youth.

The problem was his mother. Alex had not always taken the advice of doctors where Guy was concerned — oh, about his physical well-being — yes. She had carried out medical instructions meticulously, but as far as his emotional development was concerned, Alex had always known best how to give her elder son the optimum pleasure from his constrained existence . . . or she thought she had.

* * *

'I really don't see why we need to go through all this again, Paul.'

'Alex, I've become more than a doctor to your family since Guy's condition was diagnosed — at least, I hope I have — I hope I'm a friend.'

'Of course you're a friend.'

'Then please try to understand that I only have Guy's interests at heart when I tell you that he needs more freedom . . . he can't hear us from the next room, can he?'

'No — when he's asleep he's gone for the night.'

Once again, she was wrong.

'He really should be at school with Toby — he's missing out on so much — socialization in particular. And, with a few sensible precautions, there is no reason why he shouldn't lead a perfectly normal life at school — hundreds of haemophiliacs do, you know.'

'Yes, I know. You've told me before.'

'Most families can't afford a private tutor, for a start.'

'No, but we can — and Guy is going to continue his education at home.'

'Even if it means him missing out on so much? On good old fashioned fun?'

Guy, lying motionless on his bed, smiled and echoed that word in a weary whisper . . . 'fun!'

'Guy has plenty of fun at home with

me — and he loves his tutor. She's a splendid woman. He's doing very well academically.'

'Yes, I'm sure he is — he's a bright boy.'

'And what about the risks, Paul? You know what ruffians some of those children are. Suppose he cracks his head open in the playground?'

'I've explained to you before, there are special padded helmets for children like Guy. Anyway, they learn to be careful and avoid fights — and trouble in general. But if the worst came to the worst, the school would contact you immediately — and the hospital too — and Guy could have an extra injection within minutes, or any other treatment that was necessary.'

'I can't take the chance though, Paul . . . I just can't. Guy's haemophilia is particularly chronic — I don't have to tell you that. I just cannot risk him having real brain damage — or any more problems than he already has. So many things could happen to him at school.'

'You're damaging him though, Alex.

37

Life is about risks for all of us, and Guy should be living as normal a life as possible. You are harming him by over-protecting him. His emotional development is simply not normal . . . it can't be. You'll find that you're storing up real problems for Guy, problems that are surreptitiously developing now, and which will show themselves in later life.'

'He is not going to school, Paul, and that's that.'

'Something else, Alex, those rooms that you've had specially done for him, with padded furniture and no corners — that wasn't a good idea either.'

'But it gives him the freedom to move around in those rooms without fear of bruising himself. I thought you'd approve of that! It's a safe haven for him.'

'Guy might see it as a padded cell, albeit a sumptuous one.'

'Don't be ridiculous, Paul. He isn't locked in.'

'Not with a key perhaps — not physically — but . . .'

'Nothing I do is right for Guy in your eyes, is it? I only want the best for him.

I've devoted my life to making Guy happy.'

'Yes, Alex, I know. And I fear that might be part of the problem. You're suffocating him.'

'Rubbish! I'm just looking after him.'

'He needs independence. What about the injections? Have you thought any more about that?'

'Yes. Guy is not going to be taught how to inject his own factor eight . . . not while I have breath in my body and can inject him myself.'

'And what if you drop dead tomorrow?'

'Phillip and I have both made financial provision for Guy to have a live-in nurse in the event of our death.'

'But don't you see, Alex? You are sentencing Guy to dependence on other human beings. You are allowing him no real solitude and no freedom. All kinds of illnesses make it necessary for children to learn how to inject themselves — when taught at a young age, they accept the situation far more easily than adults do. Let him learn, Alex. Let him grow up able to cope with his own condition — and to be in control of his own life.'

'No. Guy will never need to do such a thing to himself. I've made sure of that.'

There was a pause, and then Guy heard the doctor employ a quieter tone.

'Alex, please don't take offence at this suggestion . . . but I think it might be a good idea if you talked to a professional yourself.'

'A psychiatrist?'

'Or possibly a psychotherapist, I'm sure that part of your problem is guilt . . . you're carrying a massive burden of guilt.'

'I've passed on a terrible illness to my first son; I think that guilt is a very normal emotion in the circumstances, don't you? And don't say that it isn't my fault. Haemophilia is a condition passed from mother to son — who else is to blame for giving him such a dreadful legacy? I don't need to see a psychiatrist — I know exactly what I have to do.'

'Because you and Guy are so close, Alex, and because you blame yourself for his condition, it is very probable that he will learn to blame you too. Children are very perceptive about such things.'

'I don't want to talk about it any more, Paul. Thanks for your concern; I know you mean well, but I can cope — really.'

★ ★ ★

'Feeling all right, son?' Phillip sat on the edge of Guy's bed.

'Yes, fine.'

'Aunt Kate's arrived and your mother sent me to tell you that Christmas lunch will be ready in half an hour precisely.'

'Great.'

'I should tidy yourself up a bit and get to the dining room pretty quick.'

'Right, Dad, I'll be there.'

Guy watched his father saunter from the room. He was a tall, strong man who oozed health from every pore, and who had always lived at a distance from his elder son.

It was perfectly understandable that Phillip should feel closer to Toby, after all, Toby had always helped in the business and would take it over in the fullness of time. Guy was not jealous of the relationship that Toby and his father enjoyed. He was aware of Phillip's pride in Toby and of their deep friendship, but he knew that his father loved him too.

Part of the problem was that Phillip could not spend a great deal of time with Guy; he was, quite naturally, fully occupied with his horses — with the improvement of the bloodline — the thoroughbred. How could an imperfect human, like himself, compete against such wonderful animals for his father's time and attention?

Guy's thoughts returned to the fish. Seeing those little prisoners, whose lives seemed useless — merely an existence — had mirrored his own plight.

One dread, in particular, lived permanently in Guy's mind. He knew that, as the joints in his knees, ankles and hips became more damaged and painful due to internal bleeding, he would have to rely more and more on his wheelchair to allow him some mobility.

The quality of his life was deteriorating quite rapidly now that he had almost reached the great age of twenty-five

— the true beginning for most.

Guy stood up and stretched his arms above his head. His sad eyes narrowed.

'Bastards!' he shouted. 'Bastards! Fish . . . bastard fish!'

Suddenly he was frantic — dizzy with rage. He blundered around his rooms like a wild animal pacing relentlessly in a cage, its mind destroyed by the restrictions inflicted on its body. He had to get out.

'I'm just going for a breath of fresh air,' he called, to anyone who happened to be in the vicinity, as he strode along the wide, oak-panelled hall which led to the back door of the mansion that was his home. 'Won't be long.'

It was a mild Christmas morning and the sun was trying to force its way through a weakening wall of cloud.

Guy walked around to the west side of Dunbar House, where dense woods hid him from view. The breeze on his face felt as though it was cleansing him. He began to run, gently at first. Pain gripped his knees and hips, but he could not stop . . . not today. Today he refused to submit to his disability. He ran faster, stumbling as the pain became stronger, but still driving himself on, his mind competing against his body for dominance. Then, suddenly, it was over. Excruciating pain forced him to the ground. Guy lay panting and sobbing among the damp, smelly leaves which had softened his fall. He pounded the ground with his fist, hoping that he would injure his hand and ruin his mother's Christmas. His frustration was intolerable.

'Guy — are you there?'

It was the unmistakable voice of Aunt Kate.

Guy wiped his tears away and sat up.

'Over here!' he called, his tone strained and pitiful.

'There you are!' she chirped. 'Are you all right, love?'

'Yes, took a bit of a tumble, that's all — tree-root I expect.'

'Any cuts or bruises?'

'No — none.'

'No — it all looks pretty soft around here — you'll live. Come on, up you get.'

Aunt Kate was no relation to the

Dunbars, but she was Alex's oldest and closest friend, and she had seen Guy and Toby grow up. Being a spinster, she had always taken a great interest in the two boys, but especially in Guy, because she was his godmother. She had, however, never fussed over him, and she held an exalted place in Guy's affections because of this. Aunt Kate had always known what Guy needed far more than his family had. He adored her.

'My legs are a bit painful,' he murmured, 'give me a minute.'

'You've been overworking them, haven't you? You look all hot and bothered. Stubborn as an ox — always were.'

'Don't grumble me, Aunt Kate.'

'Why not? What you really need is a good hiding — big as you are. Your poor mother's going frantic in there — turkey in one hand and hypodermic in the other.'

'She isn't!'

'Well — almost.' They laughed and Aunt Kate hugged her Godson.

'I felt like a breath of fresh air before lunch, that's all.'

'Yes, but you know how your mother worries about you. She's convinced herself that you're bleeding to death somewhere.'

'Aunt Kate, you're like a breath of fresh air yourself. It's so good to see you.'

'Never mind your soft-soap, young Guy. Can you get up and walk yet? I'm getting a bit old to give piggy-backs.'

Arm in arm, Aunt Kate and Guy walked back to the house, and the rest of Christmas was almost bearable.

As he lay in bed on Boxing Day morning, his limbs still aching from the previous day's madness, Guy thought of Joanna sharing her final Christmas with Ben and Samantha. He desperately wanted the holiday to be over so that he could do his work — fulfil his purpose.

'Yes, make the most of it, Joanna,' he urged in a whisper, 'I'll be seeing you soon.'

2

Tuesday, the fifth of January was the day which Guy Dunbar had chosen for the murder of Joanna Coles.

It had to be a Tuesday because her husband went out at about seven o'clock every Tuesday evening and did not return till late. Guy had learned this during his weeks of surveillance before Christmas. He did not know where Stuart Coles went to on his weekly outing — that did not matter — as long as he was not there to protect his wife.

Guy had never learned to drive a car. At the mere suggestion of him taking lessons and acquiring his own vehicle, his mother would fly into a panic and make such a drama of the whole idea that it was easier to let her drive him everywhere. Frequently, however, in order to assert his doubtful independence, Guy would insist on catching a bus into Darley New Town. This is what he had done during his

47

weeks of watching and what he did now, on the afternoon of January the fifth.

He alighted in the main street of town at about half past three. There was time to kill. Guy did not want to walk around for too long; he needed to conserve his energy for that evening. So, he went to a large, self-service restaurant and had a cup of tea.

The place was busy with afternoon shoppers. Guy stayed there for more than an hour. It was drizzling outside, and he watched as elderly ladies entered in pairs, shaking their umbrellas on the doorstep, and young, harassed mothers manoeuvred their push-chairs and whining toddlers into the warm, steamy oasis.

It amused Guy to look around at these people and wonder what their reactions would be if they knew that he was about to commit a murder. He smiled to himself. They would not understand, not these ignorant human beings. He knew that much. Their minds had been conditioned; they would think of the murder as a crime. Guy pitied them. Their most important thoughts, he mused, were probably about what to buy for tomorrow's dinner.

How could they know that he had a mission — a duty? Their lives were mundane and futile. They would be of no service to mankind — to the future, but they would learn from him . . . in time, they would all learn from him.

It was five thirty and dark when Guy left the restaurant and sauntered along the main street, zipped up sports bag in hand. The pavements were wet and the shop lights were reflected, like fuzzy, golden pools on the black, shining road.

Guy entered the telephone kiosk outside the post office and dialed the number for Dunbar House. He had purposely left his mobile at home.

'Hello.'

It was Toby's voice; Guy was relieved.

'Hi, it's me — Guy. Tell Mum that I won't be having dinner at home tonight. I fancy a curry, you know, that new place in Parade Street.'

'O.K.'

'I'll get the eight thirty bus back — all right?'

'Yes, Guy, I'll tell her. See you later — enjoy your meal.'

It was not the first time that Guy had made such a phone call, so the family would think nothing of it, except for Alex, of course, who would not rest until he was safely at home.

When Guy entered the Curry Palace in Parade Street, it was a little after six o' clock. The aroma of the place was rich and spicy, and a few early diners had already begun their meal.

Guy felt warm and relaxed as he started to eat. Life was blossoming for him . . . at last. He reflected on how careful he had been about the preparations for Joanna's death, and now the time had almost come.

It seemed so long since he had found that old knife from the stables, discarded with the rubbish. That find had aided his plans so very much. He fondly touched the sports bag by his side, which contained the said knife, now as clean as when new, and wrapped in a long, plastic mackintosh. There was also a pair of worn, leather riding gloves from the same pile of stable refuse. It had been a stumbling block for some time — how to find a knife which no one would miss, he had almost decided to buy one for the purpose, but that would have been very risky. Then, to find one that nobody wanted, and the gloves too — that was a bonus.

Guy paid for his meal and then walked out into the deserted street. It was raining quite hard now — luck was on his side. He stood in a shadowy shop doorway and unzipped his bag. Gently he took out the large, plastic mackintosh — one that he had not worn for many years and which nobody would ever expect him to wear again. It slipped on easily over his stylish leather jacket. Then he donned the old riding gloves. He felt like a tramp, but Joanna would not be commenting on his dress sense.

The walk from the centre of Darley New Town to the outskirts, where Joanna's smart, detached house nestled in the peripheral woodland of the New Forest, took about twenty-five minutes. By the time he reached the lane, from where he had so often observed his quarry, Guy's legs were quite painful. Tonight, though, he would not allow himself to think of that.

As he walked up to Joanna's front door, he noted that, just as he had expected, her husband's car was not on the drive.

He pressed the doorbell and waited. Guy had always anticipated a feeling of exhilaration when he had dreamed of this moment, but there was none. He was calm and resolute. He felt that no task would be beyond his capabilities, but that the joy would come later.

'Hello — it's Mr. Dunbar, isn't it?'

Joanna's face was radiant as she greeted him with genuine pleasure.

'Please — call me Guy.'

Joanna took the security chain — her last tangible protection — from the door. She led her visitor into a large, modern kitchen.

'I expect it's about the school's charity day next week, is it? . . . The ponies? . . . More fund raising?'

'Er . . . '

'I've just got the children to bed — will

you join me? I've put the kettle on for coffee.'

'No, not just now thanks.'

'You're very wet — give me your mackintosh.'

Joanna approached her murderer.

'No, really, I can't stay long.'

'Ben loves it when you and your mother bring the ponies to the school.'

Joanna went on in her usual enthusiastic way, as she prepared her cup of coffee. 'He's always so excited about it.' She turned to face Guy, leant back on her gleaming, white units and took a sip of her drink. 'Now, how can I help next week?'

'No — no, Mrs. Coles, I haven't actually come about the fund raising day.'

'Oh — sorry — what then?'

While Joanna had been busily talking and making her drink, Guy had retrieved the knife from his sports bag. Now, he slowly walked towards her, the weapon behind his back.

Joanna's mind teemed with fleeting and unconnected thoughts of what might be happening, as she stared, with dread, into

Guy's smiling, yet threatening eyes. An involuntary word of disbelief parted her lips as the realization gripped her heart that she was in mortal danger. She knew that she must scream, but before her voice could obey her brain, Guy's hand covered her mouth. Joanna tried desperately to fight back, but the weight of his tall body pinned her against the kitchen units. She saw the knife clutched in his left hand and terror paralyzed her.

'I'm doing this for Ben,' Guy whispered, as the cup containing the coffee was knocked from the worktop, showering the hot liquid over the floor. 'What a wonderful mother everybody thinks you are.'

The horror in Joanna's eyes now merged with absolute bewilderment. She tried to force Guy's hand from her face, grasping at a brief and barren hope that she may be able to reason with him if she could only speak. The sensation of cold steel on her neck, however, caused her to be absolutely still once more; her desire to talk to her attacker was forgotten.

Joanna felt that she would faint away if

the knife should pierce her skin, but, in the event, she did not. As Guy slowly — even gently — pushed the point of the weapon into the side of her neck, and she became aware of her warm blood trickling down to her shoulder, she felt more alive than she had ever done. Her senses appeared to be magnified and fused with fear. Not only could she feel the red strand seeping reluctantly from the, as yet, small wound, but she could smell the metallic aroma of the healthy, life-giving liquid which, a moment before had been pulsing through her veins. The tears, which almost blinded her, were hot, and they stung her eyes as the knife stung her neck. She could hear the closeness of her murderer, the crackling of the hideous plastic mackintosh and the deliberate breathing of a man possessed by an obsession.

'Poor little Ben,' Guy murmured, pushing the knife no further, 'what a life you've given him. You don't deserve to live — mothers like you.' Guy's voice was gaining strength. 'Looking after him — fussing over him — showing everybody how you care — but it's all your fault! You did it to him — you gave him his life — his abnormal, pitiful life! You sentenced him to hell! Ben would kill you if he could — but I'll do it for him!'

Now Guy was pressing so hard against Joanna's mouth with the palm of his hand that she could not avoid biting the insides of her cheeks. The steel blade sunk further into her flesh and the pain intensified. A stifled grunting sound from her throat failed to halt Guy's relentless assault.

As the knife penetrated deeper into her neck and the blood no longer seeped but oozed, Joanna's will began to fade. She knew that she was dying. There was no strength any more in her limbs. Only Guy held her on her feet.

As he pulled the knife from her neck, sticky and scarlet, and plunged it, this time quickly and with force, into her chest, Joanna's eyes ceased to function. There was nothing but blackness . . . then, there was nothing at all.

Guy's gloved hands retrieved the knife once more from Joanna's body. He stepped back, allowing her to drop to the floor, where her blood gushed, mixing with the spilled coffee like paints on an artist's palette. Next, he dropped the knife back into the open sports bag, wiped the soles of his shoes thoroughly clean on a nearby towel and put that in the bag too. Then he took off his bloody mackintosh, shook the drips into the rapidly growing warm, red puddle and pushed the soiled garment in with the knife and the towel. Being careful not to tread in the blood again, Guy took two plastic carrier bags from his pockets and put one over each of his cleaned shoes; he must leave no trace of a footprint. Guy smiled down at his victim as he removed his gloves, dropped them into the bag and turned to leave the kitchen. He walked briskly along the hall with the open bag by his side. No — he had touched nothing.

'Mummy — Mummy! Ben wants you!'

Samantha's voice echoed in Guy's head. He took a handkerchief from his jacket pocket and used it to open and close the front door with some haste.

Once the handkerchief was also in the bag, Guy walked up the empty, rain-soaked lane for a few yards. Lastly, he removed the plastic bags from over his shoes, stuffed them in with the rest of the evidence and zipped up the innocent looking receptacle.

He would not catch the bus at the nearest stop, that would be foolish, no, he would walk back to Darley New Town and catch it from there.

By the time he lowered himself heavily onto the seat of the bus, Guy's legs and hips were very painful. He felt utterly exhausted, but so satisfied and elated that he feared the other lone passenger would sense his joy, so he made a conscious effort not to smile.

As the bus bumped its way along the lanes to Dunbar House, Guy could still hear Samantha calling for her mother, and he wondered who would find Joanna. There was no remorse in his heart, though, absolutely none. He knew that he had done the right thing, and that Joanna's children would thank him for it one day — especially Ben. Yes — he had avenged poor little Ben.

No, Guy did not have to repress feelings of guilt — there simply were none.

As someone at Dunbar House may have noticed Guy leave with the sports bag, it was imperative that he should be carrying it on his return. He said a brief 'hello' to his family, who were still finishing their dinner, and then went to his rooms, where he put the bag in his wardrobe and had a wash.

'Did you buy anything in town?' Alex asked later, when Guy joined the others for coffee in the drawing room.

'No — nothing special. I had a very good meal though.'

'Alone?'

'Yes, Mother — alone. I do like to spend time on my own sometimes, you know. It makes me feel almost normal — even independent!'

'Guy!' Alex sounded hurt. 'There's no need to . . .'

'Sorry — I'm tired. I think I'll get an early night.'

Guy went to bed. His mother wiped away a tear.

* ★ ★

At three o'clock in the morning, the watch on Guy's wrist bleeped a gentle alarm. His limbs still ached from the previous evening's walking, but he had to complete his work. After dressing hurriedly, he took the sports bag and its foul contents from his wardrobe, turned off the burglar alarms and walked out of the back door and into the cold night.

The vast grounds of Dunbar House spread out for acre upon acre in all directions, but Guy was heading for one very particular place.

By now, the rain had stopped and the clear skies had brought a hard frost. The moon's stolen light allowed Guy to find his way through the still, naked trees without falling. He walked as briskly as he was able in an attempt to keep warm. Then he saw it, just ahead, the circular dry stone wall which marked the only natural well in the area. Guy sat on the wall and stared down into the blackness.

He remembered standing there with Toby when they were children, both

60

enthralled by the unknown — by the enigma of the well.

Their father had shown them how to allow a stone to drop to the bottom and listen for its arrival, so that they could perceive something of its great depth. But they had preferred to hold on to the mystery of the place, swapping ideas about what creatures could be living down there.

The well also brought back a strong sense of the forbidden to Guy, because his mother had made both her sons promise that they would not go there without her or their father. She feared that one of them might climb onto the stone wall and fall to his death. Guy could still remember the thrill when he and Toby had disobeyed her and returned to the well by themselves, on one of the rare occasions when he had escaped from the house.

The same sensation rose in him now, as he dropped the sports bag and Joanna's blood into the darkness. It seemed an age before he heard the splash. He smiled . . . it was done.

Guy walked, jubilant, back to the house and turned the burglar alarms back on. In just a few minutes he was in bed again, and in a few more, enjoying a sound slumber.

The next day would find him pondering on who his second victim would be.

3

Chief Inspector Blaire offered Stuart Coles a cigarette. With trembling hand the non-smoker took one and the gentle policeman lit it for him.

It was three o'clock in the morning and the lounge, being relatively free from forensic investigators by now, was the room in which the Chief Inspector sat with the murdered woman's husband.

A keen young Detective Sergeant looked on, noting his senior's every word. John Skinner felt honoured to work with such an acclaimed officer as Silas Blaire.

'Are you sure you wouldn't like to contact your G.P., Mr. Coles?' Chief Inspector Blaire asked quietly. 'He'd give you something for the shock.'

'No — no really — I don't like taking drugs of any kind if I can help it.'

'As you wish.'

Silas Blaire's speech was slow and deliberate. His years of experience in such circumstances enabled him to cast an air of calm in even the most dire of situations.

He was not a particularly tall man, but he was broad, and he faced the world squarely, with head high and back straight. His thick, sandy hair concealed the spattering of grey, which had only just begun to appear, and his pale blue eyes carried a certain vulnerability in their dependable gaze.

Now that he had reached his twenty-fifth year in the force, there was nothing which could shock him, though much that he saw still pained him. He had become accustomed to murder and misery, but had never been able to toughen himself against such things. Beneath his composure was a great sorrow and infinite compassion.

'Is she still there, Chief Inspector?' Stuart cleared his throat. The alien smoke was irritating him so he stubbed out the half-finished cigarette. 'Is she still on the kitchen floor? Still lying there?'

'We have to give the forensic chaps time to do their work, Mr. Coles.'

'Was she . . . was she . . . ?'

'From our first impressions, there was no sexual assault.'

Stuart Coles nodded slowly.

'What are they doing to her?' he blurted, as though he was afraid of the reply.

'They can learn a great deal from your wife's surroundings, clothing and so on, but the police pathologist will be attending to your wife's body . . . he is a doctor.'

'Yes of course.'

'You see, she still has a lot to tell us.'

Stuart found kindness in the policeman's eyes.

'Poor Joanna,' he murmured.

'You do want us to find your wife's murderer, don't you, Mr. Coles?'

'Strangely enough, I don't much care,' Stuart whispered, his red eyes moistening again. 'Won't bring her back, will it? I've lost her . . . we've lost her.'

'It might stop another family going through what you're feeling now though, sir.'

'Yes, I realize that. I suppose I'm being

selfish, but at this moment I don't care about anybody else — I just want this torment to be over.'

'I understand that — I really do, but now that your mother and father have taken the children to their home, we will need to talk, Mr. Coles.'

'Yes — you want to question me. I suppose the husband is the number one suspect in these cases.' Stuart ran his slender fingers through his fair, wavy hair.

'What time did you arrive home from your squash club, Mr. Coles?' The Chief Inspector's voice was quiet, but there was an authority in his tone which could be neither concealed nor ignored.

'Er — eleven o' clock — ten past — something like that — the same as usual.'

'If you could be as precise as possible when answering my questions, sir,' the Chief Inspector urged, 'it's surprising how the smallest detail can be of the greatest importance.'

'Christ!' Stuart shouted, thumping his chair with his clenched fist. 'It was about eleven o' clock, but it could have been ten past! Silly of me, but I didn't look at my watch when I found my wife lying murdered — I suppose I should have done, but it completely slipped my mind!'

Chief Inspector Blaire pursed his lips and bowed his head, giving Stuart time to recover from his outburst.

'Now, Mr. Coles,' the policeman continued after a few minutes of meditation, 'you went to play squash on the same day and at the same time each week — is that correct?'

'Yes.' Stuart was subdued now, like a child who had expected a rebuke, but suffered greater remorse because of its absence.

'So, quite a few people would have known that your wife would be alone earlier this evening?'

'Well, yes, I suppose so — anyone who knew my habits.'

'Was your wife careful about using the security chain on the front door, Mr. Coles?'

'Yes, she was. She always used it when she was alone with the children.'

'She told you that?'

'She didn't have to. When I left the house for any reason, she used to come to the front door with me, and as I turned to walk up the garden path, I could hear the sliding noise that the chain lock made. And she always had to come and take the chain off when I came home.'

'Did you hear her lock the door behind you tonight, Mr. Coles?'

Stuart frowned.

'Yes — yes, I did.'

'Are you certain of that?'

'Absolutely. I got into the habit of listening for that noise — one of those things you do without actually thinking about it. If I hadn't heard it, I would have reminded her to put the chain on — called through the letterbox, but there was no need to remind her tonight. She definitely locked it.'

'So, when you came home at around eleven o' clock, Mr. Coles, did you knock or ring — thinking that the chain would be across the door?'

'No — I always put my key in the lock and turned it, so that Joanna would know it was me. Once she heard the door open a fraction and I spoke to her, she would shut the door again and undo the chain. I never rang the bell, it might have woken the children.'

'But tonight?'

'Tonight, when I unlocked the door and pushed it, expecting the chain to be there, the door just opened wide.'

'Did this alarm you — or make you suspicious at all?'

'Yes, it did. I remember calling Joanna's name directly I was in the hall.'

Stuart Coles closed his eyes momentarily and sighed a deep, trembling sigh. 'I thought that something must be wrong — but I didn't expect . . . '

'No, of course not.' Silas Blaire gave Stuart time to recover. 'So, if your wife was not the kind of woman to take the security chain off the door and allow a stranger into the house when she was alone at night, we can assume that . . . '

'That this maniac was someone she knew.'

'It does seem very likely, Mr. Coles. There was no sign of a forced entry. Your wife removed the security chain herself.'

'My God!'

'Can you think of anyone, anyone at all, who might have wanted to harm Mrs. Coles?'

'No — no one — absolutely not.'

'I'm afraid that that is always the first reaction to that question in these cases, Mr. Coles.'

'I'm telling you, Chief Inspector, she had no enemies.'

'No, but bear with me for a minute, will you. The person who killed your wife had planned to do so. We have gathered that much already: the fact that he or she came when you would be out — the way the murderer cleaned himself up and got out of the house without leaving obvious clues to his identity — the kind of clues we would have found immediately if the attack had been spontaneous and frenzied — these things tell us that the murder was pre-meditated.'

'Yes. It's difficult to believe, but I understand what you're saying.'

'Nothing seems to have been taken, as you've seen, so the motive wasn't robbery. The killer, therefore, is very likely unhinged — obsessive or deranged in some way. Now, you say that your wife had no enemies, but can you think of anyone who might have allowed something in their mind to get out of all proportion — something that, to the rest of us, might seem minor — even trivial? For example, did anyone ever appear jealous of your wife in any way? Is there anybody who might have born a grudge — over a matter of little importance perhaps? It could be something that happened years ago, Mr. Coles. You'd be amazed at the things that fester in people's minds.'

'Amazed? Yes, I suppose I would be.' Utter exhaustion half-closed Stuart's eyes. 'I don't feel able to cope with any more of this at the moment, Chief Inspector Blaire.'

'No, of course not. That'll do for now. I'd like you to contact me, though, if anyone does spring to mind. Give it some thought, eh?'

'I shall think of little else.'

★   ★   ★

Dorothy Ballard sat in the staff room of Darley Hill Special School, looking stunned and incredulous.

'I just can't take it in, Chief Inspector Blaire,' she said drying a tear. 'I've been Ben's teacher since September, and in that time Joanna has become a friend. Why would anyone want to do a dreadful thing like that? It's unbelievable.'

'You've never heard anybody — another of the parents — anyone at all — speak as though they disliked Mrs. Coles?'

'No never. She was very popular.'

'Did you see very much of Mr. Coles?'

'No, not much at all. Joanna and I used to have a chat most days — about what Ben had been doing and so on — but Mr. Coles was at work, I think.'

'When was the last time you saw Joanna Coles?'

'I expected to see her this morning, Chief Inspector, it being the first day of the new term, but . . . er . . . it was the party . . . the day we broke up for the Christmas holidays.'

'And you noticed nothing unusual about her? Or anyone she came into contact with at the party?'

'Nothing unusual at all. Mind you, it was all very hectic, as you can imagine.'

'Did Mrs. Coles have any special friends among the other parents, Mrs. Ballard?'

'I can't think of anyone in particular, Chief Inspector. She was friendly with everyone really.'

'Who did she sit with at the Christmas party — can you remember?'

The teacher's eyes widened.

'Yes — yes — it was Michael Gilchrist — and . . . ' She stopped short. She was clearly troubled and reluctant to go on.

'And?' Chief Inspector Blaire exhibited great patience.

'No, it's nothing.' Mrs. Ballard shook her head.

'Tell me about it please.' The policeman's persuasive tone was not enough to tempt Mrs. Ballard into confiding in him.

'It really isn't of any importance, Chief Inspector, and the wrong word from me might cause trouble for the poor man. He has enough to cope with looking after Giles.'

'I don't have to remind you that this is

73

a murder enquiry, do I, Mrs. Ballard?' Silas Blaire's voice was suddenly commanding and urgency bit into his words.

John Skinner was impressed by his boss's cool control of the interview.

'It's nothing — honestly,' she answered dismissively, 'it was just a little flirtation — the Christmas spirit, I expect.'

'At the Christmas party?'

'Yes. He — Mr. Gilchrist — put his hand on Joanna's knee. I remember, because it made me chuckle at the time — the look she gave him. I was standing right behind them. I couldn't help but notice what happened. She soon moved away from him — left him in no doubt that his advances weren't welcome.'

'I see.'

'Please don't read anything into what I've just told you, Chief Inspector. It was obviously a spur of the moment thing — there was no harm done and none intended, I'm sure. Michael Gilchrist is a very good man. He looks after his disabled son alone, you know.'

'Does he really?'

'Yes, he's devoted to the boy.'

'And his wife?'

'Er, she left him, I believe. Some people just can't cope with a badly handicapped child. There are all kinds of problems and sacrifices. You can't possibly understand if you haven't faced the tragedy of such a situation.'

'No, I'm sure you're right.'

* * *

John Skinner's buoyant personality, modish appearance and handsome face made him a turner of all female heads. He had so far avoided marriage, however, enjoying instead the bachelor existence and harbouring no ambitions to make that short, but crucial excursion up the aisle to the altar.

'Have you got any children, sir?' he asked Silas Blaire as he drove him back to the police station, the pupils of the school still prevailing in his mind.

'Yes, one son.'

'How old?'

'Twenty — er — twenty-two now.'

'Is he in the force — following in

father's footsteps?'

'Good God no.' Chief Inspector Blaire smiled an empty smile. 'I've hardly seen him in the last three years. He lives with my father.'

'Oh, I see.'

'No, you don't, Sergeant Skinner, you don't see at all.'

'No, sir.'

'My father is Sir Benjamin Blaire.' Silas waited for a reaction, but none was immediately forthcoming. 'You know — the newspaper magnate.'

'Oh — him!' John Skinner was clearly in awe. 'He's your father?'

'That's right.'

'But he's . . . '

'Worth a bob or two — let's leave it at that, shall we? I always find talking in millions depressing somehow.'

'Damned if I do! What the hell are you doing earning a living? You've no need to work . . . er . . . sir.' The Sergeant reminded himself that Silas Blaire was his senior officer, even if he had no need to be in the force at all.

'My father is a first class bastard,

Skinner, he always has been. He's a self-made man. I suppose that should warrant some kind of admiration, but it doesn't — not from me anyway. I know him far too well. We rowed from the moment I was old enough to recognize all the greed and selfishness that emanates from him. All he cares about are his possessions — and while I lived under his roof I was just another of those possessions. How do you think I got such a bloody stupid name as Silas?'

'I had wondered, sir,' Skinner replied, not quite managing to conceal a grin.

'My father considered the name to be 'stylish' and to be admirably suitable for a young man destined to live unprecariously at the top of the social ladder.'

'Well — I don't know of any yobs called Silas, I must admit. So you didn't get on then — you and your father?'

'As soon as I was old enough, I got out — rebelled and left home. I just couldn't live with him any longer. It would have been different if my mother had lived, but she died when I was ten. He broke her heart — women — you know, the old story. It must have been his money the tarts were after; no one could have loved him for himself.'

'Not even your mother?'

'Yes, she did. That was before he made his millions though. She always told me that he had been different in his youth. It was as if she felt she should try to excuse his behaviour — even to me — especially to me. Anyway, to cut a long story short, I didn't have any contact with him for years. He was horrified when I joined the police force. He didn't even come to my wedding — not that I was worried about that. After James was born, though, he used to visit us from time to time — another potential possession, you see.'

'Oh — your son.'

'His grandson! I tried to let James know what his grandfather was really like, but that seemed to turn him against me rather than my father. I handled it all very badly — I must have done. In the end, James went to live in luxury with grandpa. I don't know whether it was the pull of all that money, my father wooing him away or my own stupidity that caused him to go. Anyway, he went.'

'Oh dear.'

'I don't think I'm very good at personal relationships, Skinner. A year after James left, my wife went to. She spends quite a lot of time at my father's apparently. She says it's so that she can be with James, but the old man looks after her financially. She certainly doesn't get enough from me to keep her in the expensive clothes — or to run her bloody Porsche. He's bought them both, my wife and my son.'

'So you live on your own, sir?'

'That's it, Skinner! No one to fight with — it's bliss!'

* * *

'This has been such a shock, Chief Inspector,' Jean Barnett explained, her damp handkerchief clutched in her restless fingers.

'Yes, I'm sure it has, Mrs. Barnett.'

'It wasn't as if we just worked together — we were friends. Peter, that's my husband, and myself used to meet Joanna and Stuart socially. We'd often spend the

79

evening at their house. It had to be there because they didn't like leaving Ben. Poor Ben — and Samantha too. Whatever will Stuart do?'

'It'll take him time to sort that out — it's early days yet. The children are with their grandparents.'

'That must be Stuart's mother and father; Joanna's parents died when she was young.'

'Yes, that's right.'

'Poor Stuart.'

Jean whimpered into her hanky again. Her hazel eyes were swollen from crying, but Silas Blaire could not fail to notice her attractive, though mature features and her well-preserved figure. Jean's thick, chestnut hair was short and styled, and the Chief Inspector stared for a moment at its seductive shine.

'So, you knew both Joanna and Stuart Coles very well, Mrs. Barnett?'

'Yes. I spent a lot more time with Joanna, naturally, but I know Stuart fairly well too. He must be devastated. They were a really happy couple — even with their problems.'

'Ben, you mean?'

'Yes. I think he made the bond between Joanna and Stuart exceptionally strong.'

'Have you seen them since Christmas?'

'Yes, we spent New Year's Eve with them. Nothing very exciting, you understand. We just went round and shared a few drinks — Joanna had made a little buffet — it was all very pleasant. My God, that was just a few days ago and now . . .'

'It's a good thing we don't know what's in store for us, I always think.'

'Absolutely.'

'So everything at the Coles's house was as you would have expected — no bad atmospheres between Stuart and Joanna?'

'No, Chief Inspector, nothing!' Jean's eyes were suddenly intense with disbelief as well as sorrow. 'You don't think that Stuart killed her, do you?' she asked, her tone mocking such a suggestion.

'We have no firm suspects as yet, Mrs. Barnett. These questions do have to be asked.'

'Yes, I'm sure they do, but you're going in completely the wrong direction there.

Stuart adored Joanna.'

'Strangely enough, I've met many adoring husbands who've murdered their wives — quite a thought that, isn't it?'

Jean averted her eyes from the policeman's compelling stare.

'Yes,' she answered quietly, almost apologetically, 'not Stuart, though, it just couldn't have been Stuart.'

'Did Mrs. Coles ever talk to you about anyone who disliked her? Someone who bore a grudge perhaps.'

'No, no, I can't think of anyone at all. Everybody liked Joanna immensely. She was a very charming and friendly woman.'

Sergeant Skinner left the office of the grammar school to answer a call on his mobile.

'A message, sir,' he whispered, when Silas joined him in the lobby, 'from the lads at the Coles's house. They've found a letter in her dressing table drawer — a personal letter — to Joanna from Peter Barnett.'

'So, Mr. Barnett,' the Chief Inspector said darkly, as he handed Peter the letter, 'you sent this to the murdered woman about a month ago.'

The huge form of Peter Barnett sank into his armchair as he took the folded paper. He was a good-looking man with dark hair which was elegantly streaked with silver at the temples, and brown eyes that openly revealed apprehension at the thought of what the Inspector might have inferred from this wretched letter.

'Yes, I did. I wish to God she'd destroyed it. Nothing ever came of it — it was stupid — ridiculous — I should never have written the damned thing.'

'Will you tell me about your relationship with Joanna Coles, Mr. Barnett. I want to know everything there is to know, please. Not because I'm nosey, you understand, but because we have a woman who's been brutally murdered, and in order to find her killer, we must have a complete picture of that woman's life.'

'Yes, I know, Chief Inspector.' Peter returned the letter to Silas Blaire. 'Thank you for arranging this meeting for this afternoon, while Jean is at work. She doesn't know anything about this note.'

'We try to be as discreet as possible, Mr. Barnett, but I can't promise that your wife will be kept in ignorance about it.'

'I see. I hope to God she is.'

'Now, you and Joanna Coles?'

'No, Chief Inspector, not me and Joanna Coles — it was never that. What a bloody fool I was to write to her. You see, Jean and I used to go round and spend the occasional evening with Stuart and Joanna. They couldn't go out much because of their boy, and they hadn't been in the area all that long. We just became friends, the four of us. Jean and Joanna got on like a house on fire, and Stuart's a good sort too. It suited all of us to meet socially. Our only daughter has just gone off to university and we've been feeling a bit lost.'

'Go on.'

'Well, Joanna was quite a looker, Chief Inspector Blaire. We all notice these things, don't we?'

'Indeed we do, Mr. Barnett.'

'Well, I began to — how shall I put it?'

'As bluntly as possible please, Mr. Barnett.'

Peter stared at the senior policeman for a moment, and then at his sergeant.

'I suppose I fancied her,' he admitted, with a shrug of his broad shoulders and a jerk of his head. 'I mean, don't get the wrong idea about me, please, I have never been unfaithful to my wife. I've never written such a letter before either, in the whole of our marriage.'

'No, but in this one, you do ask to meet Joanna secretly. You say that you want to talk to her alone. Why, Mr. Barnett?'

'Christ knows!' Peter threw his head back and sighed sharply. 'It was a whim,' he went on, with evident self-loathing. 'I kept thinking about her. Twenty-five years of marriage, I suppose — a sort of boredom. Not that I'm making excuses for my stupidity, but I just . . . wanted to be with her. Anyway, one afternoon at work, after a business lunch and far too many glasses of wine, I wrote this note and posted it. Later that evening, when I was sober again, I wished like hell that I hadn't, but it was too late then, of course.

I felt such a fool. I dreaded the next time I'd see Joanna; I knew I wouldn't be able to look her in the eye. It's the usual story, isn't it? Middle-aged man — male menopause — fancies his chances with a good-looking young woman. I was so ashamed of myself.' Peter Barnett's eyes became suddenly tearful. 'I need not have worried,' he explained, 'Joanna had so much good sense — bless her. She turned up at my office one morning — she'd been to see the dentist and had an hour off work. I didn't feel embarrassed. I expected to, but I didn't when it came to it. She was so understanding. 'I'll bet you wish you hadn't written it now, don't you?' she said, but so warmly — sympathetically — she was that kind of woman. She told me that she loved Stuart and she knew that I loved Jean. I was so relieved. Then she said that we should both forget all about my note and continue being friends, just like before. She said that, as far as she was concerned, my letter had never been written. And that, Chief Inspector Blaire, was the end of the matter. The next time we all met at the

Coles's house, Joanna was her usual self. It was never mentioned again.'

'I see,' Silas Blaire nodded slowly. 'The trouble, Mr. Barnett, though I thank you for your frankness, is that we only have your word for all this.'

'I know, but it's the truth.'

'If your proposition meant as little to Joanna Coles as you say, why didn't she throw that letter away immediately, leaving no trace of the business at all? Any thoughts, Mr. Barnett?'

'None at all, Chief Inspector. I was amazed when your men found she still had it. Perhaps she meant to throw it away, but hadn't got round to doing it. It wasn't exactly a love letter, was it? I only asked to meet her alone, after all.'

'Mm. And what about Stuart Coles — did he know about this letter?'

'Well no, I'm sure he didn't. He never said anything — I mean he would have shown some anger, wouldn't he, if he'd seen it?'

'Exactly, Mr. Barnett.' Silas raised his eyebrows ominously.

'You're not suggesting that Stuart

found the letter, imagined that there was an affair, and murdered Joanna because he was jealous, are you?'

'It's happened before, Mr. Barnett, many times.'

'But I thought Stuart was playing squash when Joanna was murdered. His friends at the club would be his alibi, surely.'

'The time of death was early evening, he could have killed his wife and then gone straight to the squash club.'

'Never. Stuart would not have done such a thing — never. He just isn't the sort of person who could murder anyone, let alone his wife.'

'And what were you doing yesterday evening, Mr. Barnett?'

'What? Well, I was here — watching the television — all evening.'

'With Mrs. Barnett?'

'Yes — well no — not all the time. Jean went to see her aunt for a couple of hours — she's in an old people's home.'

'What time was that?'

'Er, she left just before seven and got back at about nine.'

'I see.'

Peter Barnett stood up, as if his substantial height might afford him some psychological advantage. It did not.

'Look, I was here,' he asserted, and then more quietly, 'I suppose I'm a suspect too — just because of that bloody letter.'

'We must examine all possibilities, Mr. Barnett.' The Chief Inspector's words were well practised — well worn on his lips. 'There are many avenues to explore in such cases.'

'Well, this avenue will take you to a dead-end, Chief Inspector Blaire. I was nowhere near Joanna Coles's house last night. Why would I be? I told you, we meant nothing to each other — all we had was friendship.'

'And I told you, Mr. Barnett, that I only have your word for that.'

'You think that Joanna and I had been having an affair?'

'Two main possibilities spring to mind, Mr. Barnett. One is that you had indeed been having an affair and Joanna wanted to end it. She may have threatened to tell

89

your wife or her husband — or both. It's a common enough scenario. You had to shut her up.'

'Rubbish!'

'The second possibility is that Joanna did come to you and put you very decisively in your place about your letter and its implications, but that you did not react to her answer in the way you would have me believe.'

'Mm?'

'Perhaps your feelings for Joanna were not as simple as you suggest, Mr. Barnett. A lot of men fancy women that they know, but they don't usually write them letters trying to arrange a secret meeting. That sounds a bit more than 'fancying' to me — that sounds like infatuation. You wanted her enough to write to her — possibly you were becoming obsessive about her — perhaps you just had to have her, Mr. Barnett.'

Silas Blaire quite suddenly resembled an outraged bull, and Sergeant Skinner made a mental note not to cross this usually placid man, as his wrath was clearly something to be avoided.

'No — no, it wasn't like that!' Peter Barnett argued.

'Then, when she refused you, you felt cheated and rejected — even worse — humiliated. Your male pride was torn apart. You were jealous of her and Stuart. Your calm exterior was hiding a churning mass of emotions — all of them negative and intensely painful.'

'You couldn't have got it more wrong, Chief Inspector Blaire.'

'Good, then you have nothing to worry about, have you, Mr. Barnett?'

The calm returned to Silas as quickly as it had left him.

* * *

'I can't spare you long, Chief Inspector,' Michael Gilchrist explained, as he returned his ironing board to the kitchen. 'I've got to pick my son up from school quite soon.'

'It'll only take a couple of minutes, Mr. Gilchrist, just a few quick questions, if you don't mind.'

The wiry young man showed Silas

91

Blaire and John Skinner into his cluttered but clean dining room. He was not handsome, and his thin face seemed permanently steeped in anxiety.

'I didn't know Joanna Coles very well, I'm afraid,' he said. 'I don't think I'll be much help to you.' He sat down at this dining table, facing the two policemen. 'It's a terrible thing, isn't it? You read about murders in the paper, but when it's on your doorstep, it really knocks you for six.'

'Your son goes to the same school as Mrs. Coles's son, Ben, is that right?'

'Yes, Darley Hill Special School. Giles is severely handicapped.'

'Just how well did you know Mrs. Coles?'

'Well, I used to chat to her, while we waited for the boys to finish school — like I chat to the other parents.'

'Were you on first name terms?'

'Yes — most of us are — it's a very friendly school — parents and teachers, we're all on first name terms. There's a lot of empathy between us, because of the problems we share in bringing up our children, I suppose.'

'Yes, that's only to be expected. And when did you last see Mrs. Coles?'

'Er, that would be the Christmas party — the last afternoon of the term.'

'Did you speak to her?'

'I should think so, I must have done — we were all talking — you know what kids' parties are like.'

'Yes, but did you have a conversation that you can remember — anything special?'

'No — nothing like that, not that I can think of.'

'Did you find Mrs. Coles attractive, Mr. Gilchrist?'

'Well yes, I should think any man would find her attractive — she was attractive.'

'Did you ever make a pass at her?'

'No!'

'Are you sure about that?'

'I'm not in the habit of making passes at married women, Chief Inspector Blaire.'

'No, perhaps not, but you were seen touching Joanna Coles's knee at the

Christmas party.'

'What?'

'So, were you making a pass at her or not?'

'Definitely not. We were all friendly that afternoon — friendlier than usual because it was almost Christmas, you know what it's like. I don't even remember touching her knee — but if I did, it was a harmless show of friendship. There was certainly nothing serious about it.'

'You've lived alone as a single parent for some time, I believe, Mr. Gilchrist.'

'Yes, a few years now.'

'You must get lonely, or do you have a regular girlfriend?'

'No, I don't have much of a social life, not with Giles — no opportunity to meet anyone.'

'Not really natural for a man to live like that, is it, Mr. Gilchrist? Almost monk-like.'

'I don't know what you're getting at, but there was nothing between Joanna and myself — nothing at all.'

'You would have liked there to be something between you though, wouldn't you?'

'I didn't try anything on with her, really. You must believe me, I'm not that sort of man. If a woman's married, then that's it — end of story — friends, but nothing more.'

'Were those two women in Potters Bar married, Mr. Gilchrist? What was it — ten years ago?'

'For God's sake! What have you raked that up for?'

'Routine check for a police record, that's all. We didn't have to look very hard. Conviction for indecent exposure.'

'So?'

'So, do your sexual urges occasionally get out of control?' Sergeant Skinner glimpsed Blaire the bull again. 'Were you so frustrated by Mrs. Coles's rejection of your advances that you were compelled to get your own back on her? Are you turned on by murder, Mr. Gilchrist? Many people are, you know.'

'Well, I'm not! I was here with Giles yesterday evening — like I always am.'

'Giles was in bed?'

'Yes. I watched television. I can tell you what was on and what happened in each

95

programme. As for Potters Bar, I was out of my head — drunk. I don't even remember what happened. It was my best mate's stag night. I would never have done anything like that if I'd been sober. These things happen when you're as drunk as I was that night, Chief Inspector Blaire. I'm not a nutter who confuses murder and sex, so you can forget that one, all right? Now, you must excuse me, I have to meet my son.'

The policemen were shown the door and Michael Gilchrist went to meet Giles.

'What we get up to when we've had a few too many eh, Skinner?' Silas Blaire remarked as he got into the police car.

'The demon drink, sir.'

'Mm — or just a bloody good excuse.'

4

The conservatory at the rear of Dunbar House was spacious and warm. It was Alex Dunbar's favourite place in winter because the multifarious plants which adorned it reminded her that spring would soon oust those grey January days and the depressing ambience which they bred.

'I didn't actually know the woman, Kate,' she explained to her best friend, as they sat in the comfortable, wicker chairs absently surveying the prolific greenery. 'I must have seen her, though, the number of times we've taken the ponies to the school. Most of the parents turn up, especially when we do our Saturday visits.'

'Must have been a madman.'

'Oh yes, must have been.'

'Well, I for one will feel a damned sight safer when they've caught him. You don't know where he's going to turn up next, do you? They don't usually stop at one.'

'No, I suppose not, unless it was someone who had a grudge against that particular woman.'

'Must have been a pretty hefty grudge, Alex.'

'Well yes — quite.'

'Of course, it's different for you, you don't live alone.'

'Look, if you feel nervous, Kate, move in here until the dreadful business is over.'

'I'm not normally the nervous type, but I'll keep your offer in mind — we'll see how things go.' Kate craned her neck and looked through the profusion of leaves and out towards the stables. 'Isn't that Toby?' she asked, squinting.

'Yes, of course it is.'

'I didn't recognize him for the minute. Is he growing his hair?'

'Well he hasn't said as much, but by the look of him I think he must be.'

'That's a shame; it's always suited him short.'

'Mm. Between you and me, Kate, I think there's an external influence.'

'A girl, you mean?'

'You've got it in one.'

'Special is she?'

'I get the feeling she is, yes. Oh, he hasn't brought her home yet, but he lets little things drop. I think she's special all right.'

'He's grown into a fine chap, Alex.'

'Yes. I look at him sometimes and feel so thankful that I had him. If I'd known about Guy's haemophilia before I conceived Toby, he wouldn't have been here. I could never have knowingly taken the risk of inflicting Guy's misery on another child. I've never prayed as much as I did during that second pregnancy, Kate. It's a wonder he did turn out normal, the state I was in. We were so lucky that he didn't inherit it like poor Guy did.'

'Yes, but don't talk as though Guy has nothing but misery in his life, Alex. It isn't true.'

'I bought him some oil paints and canvasses yesterday — I thought it might make up for that awful business with the fish tank.'

'Good idea. He used to do a lot of painting a few years back, didn't he?

99

Quite a good artist, our Guy.'

'Mm. He seemed to lose interest for some time; I hoped the new canvasses might motivate him — it seems to have worked. He's doing a still life at the moment.'

'Sounds promising. I must go in and have a look.' Kate turned somewhat tentatively to Alex. 'Before I do though,' she said, 'have you talked to him about getting a job yet?'

'He doesn't need to, Kate.'

'I know that! We've been through all this before, Alex.' Kate's expressive face registered desperation. 'He may not need to earn money, but he does need to be occupied. Painting pictures is fine for a hobby, but he needs to feel useful.'

'I don't think it troubles Guy all that much — whether he's useful or not.'

'Well, I think you're wrong. He should have something more than hobbies to keep him busy. Can't he do some of the administration for this place? There must be a lot of paperwork. I know Phillip's got a secretary, but couldn't he make Guy a manager or something? It would give him

100

more in common with Toby and his father if he were really concerned with the running of the business. He'd feel a part of things, wouldn't he? You must see that that would be good for him, Alex.'

'I agree.'

'Well then?'

'Phillip asked him to become a partner in the business, Kate, but he refused.'

'Really? I'm amazed.'

'I'm not. It's exactly what I expected. Guy knew that he wasn't really needed. He saw through it straight away. He said that we wanted him to feel useful — I think he felt patronized instead.'

'Oh dear.'

'Yes, Kate. You see, I really do understand Guy better than anyone else does. Everybody has his interests at heart, I'm sure, but I do know what's best for him.'

'That gold capella you painted this morning has turned out beautifully, Guy,' Alex enthused, as she prepared to give him his injection of factor eight.

'I thought it would make a change from the tedious bowl of fruit.'

'Well, quite.' She held the syringe up to eye level and tapped it with the confidence of a professional. 'Why don't you get out into the grounds and do some landscapes, darling? You painted one or two excellent views a while back, didn't you?'

'Yes, I might, when the weather gets warmer.'

Alex cleaned Guy's skin with cold, damp cotton wool.

'Aunt Kate looks very well, I thought,' she babbled on, 'constitution of an ox, that one.'

The needle approached Guy's skin. He closed his eyes and was suddenly a child again.

* * *

His legs, still bearing the chubbiness of the early years, were stretched out in front of him.

'Look at Donald Duck on your wallpaper,' Alex was saying, 'see if you can find Mickey Mouse for me, Guy — where is he now?'

'No!' His young voice reverberated again inside his skull. 'I don't want the needle, Mummy — give it to Toby — it's his turn!'

'Don't shout, darling, please, you've got to have your injection. Be a good boy for Mummy.'

'No — no!'

The screaming became so shrill that his mother winced, and his movements so violent that she could not hold him down without the danger of bruising him.

'If you keep still, Guy, it's over in a second, but you must keep still — please.'

'I won't! Take that away!'

He lashed out to try and knock the syringe from Alex's hand, just as his father entered the room to investigate the noise.

'Oh, Phillip — thank goodness. Give me a hand here, will you? The quicker the better.'

'Come on, Guy,' his father urged, forcing his son's legs down, as gently as he could, onto the bed, 'it won't take a minute — there's a good boy.'

The long, silver needle pierced Guy's

already sore thigh. He relaxed his hot, sticky limbs. Fighting was useless now — it was done — until the next time.

'Now, what was that all about?' Alex whispered, as she held her son close to her. 'You were such a good boy yesterday. It's like the doctor said, darling, if you don't have these little injections, you'll be very poorly. Now, you must be a sensible boy for Mummy — you really must.'

Guy could feel again Alex's soft, warm body against his vulnerable child's form. Her reddened lips left a blood-coloured smudge on his sweaty forehead. He wanted her to hold him forever against her full, bulbous breasts — to protect him from the great injustice in his life, which hurt him far more than any needle.

It was clear in his child's mind that his mother loved him, and that his injections must be necessary, but his arrant loathing of her was out of his control. She did not protect him from his illness; she was his strongest link with it.

★　★　★

104

'Guy . . . Guy . . . are you all right, darling?'

The boy inside the man recoiled at the sound of his mother's voice and hated her beautiful gentleness, but the man smiled adoringly:

'Yes, fine thanks, Mother — didn't feel a thing,' he joked.

Alone in his rooms, Guy wondered how many syringes full of factor eight his mother had pumped into his defective body over the years. It was the cheerful conversation which accompanied each and every needle that made him want to snatch the syringe from her hand, and drive it into her aging neck.

She did seem to understand that he still hated the revolting ritual, however. Everybody else assumed that he was so accustomed to injections that they no longer bothered him — familiarity breeding oblivion — everybody else was wrong though. Each needle sickened him as much as the one before had done, and as much as the next one would do. Alex knew it. She knew everything about Guy . . . no . . . she only thought she did.

5

Janice Perry would be Guy's second victim. He had decided that it would be her when accompanying his mother to the Forest Home for Handicapped Children.

It was Alex's first visit to this particular institution. There she was, wellington boots and hooded anorak, giving rides on plodding ponies to the poor little beings who lived in the home. Guy looked on, ostensibly with pride.

It was two other women who had sealed Janice's fate for her, carers who worked with the children.

'You see that common piece over there,' the short, dumpy one had said, 'that's little Andrew Perry's mother.'

Guy, who was standing close to the women, listened with fervent, but hidden interest.

'I didn't know he had a mother,' said slightly taller and dumpier carer.

'Well, he might as well not have her, the number of times she visits him. It's his birthday today — that's the only time she comes — once a year. He didn't even go home at Christmas. She worked all over the holidays, she was telling me, in that new nightclub — Dandy's.'

'Poor little kid. Fancy being here all over Christmas. She's only young herself, though, isn't she? You can see that much through all the makeup.'

'Yes, she can only have been sixteen or seventeen when she had him.'

'No age, is it?'

'No. Matron told me once that he'd have been up for adoption if he hadn't had so many problems. But as things are, this is the best place for him.'

'No father, I suppose?'

'Vanished, I think. That's men for you.'

'Mind you, in her position, a lot of people would do what she's done. Married women with supportive families would've found Andrew a handful, wouldn't they? And at least she's trying to earn a living.'

'Oh yes. I just wish she would visit him

more often — take him to her place for a while.'

'Mm. Me too.'

Guy looked at Andrew's mother, who was standing on the other side of the small field that was the makeshift paddock. He would not find out her Christian name until the serious stalking had begun — but that was her — she would be the next mother to die in the cause of justice.

Janice Perry was about five feet five and had so little flesh on her bones that she appeared skinny rather than slim. Her long, mousy brown hair had been streaked, and it hung, with greasy roots and split ends, half way down her back. Harsh, grey eyes peered through layers of black makeup, and mauve lips pouted habitually, though more from an innate ferocity than the longing to be kissed. The blue jeans, which Janice wore, were very tight and her tasty, leather jacket put the finishing touches to her tasteless and somewhat pitiful appearance.

★ ★ ★

In fact, Janice Perry was just twenty-four. She had given birth to Andrew when she was seventeen, and not long out of a children's home herself.

Janice had been placed in the care of the county when her mother departed the marital home, leaving her drunken father to beat his only child whenever he was so inclined. Once out of the institution, she had fallen pregnant by the first young man to show her what she had hoped was affection.

Being seventeen and alone in the world was enough to cope with, but giving birth to a handicapped child was simply too much. Janice had decided on freedom, and, as soon as she was able, had placed Andrew in the Forest residential home. It was the best thing for her and her son — she knew that. Her own mother had not been the kind of role model to inspire a maternal instinct.

With her bar-work, and a little prostitution thrown in, Janice made just enough money to pay for her bed-sit, which was over a small grocer's shop in Darley New Town.

She did not know whether she loved her child or not; she never allowed herself to think of such things. The tiny seed of pain which was planted inside her at their parting must not be allowed to grow. Andrew was better off where he was. Janice, who was permanently on valium plus forty cigarettes a day, would scarcely have had the patience to bring up an able-bodied child, let alone a disabled one.

'I'd have killed the poor little sod,' she would mutter to herself when any sign of a conscience reared its intrusive head. 'Bundle of nerves — that's me — no patience at all.'

Four years before Guy's interest in her, Janice had told her few friends and her landlord that Andrew had died. She had feigned grief for a week or two but, in truth, had felt relief because the interminable questions about his welfare had ended. So, as no one in her circle of acquaintances knew that Andrew still existed, she was able to forget all about him — except for those times, which came every single day, when she saw his face in her sad mind's eye.

On his birthday, however, she would take him a gift. She did not want to touch him or cuddle him or anything like that; she might not be able to let go again. It was after that annual visit that her past was not so easy to expel.

For a few hours she would think of the people she had loved, but who had not loved her. That was difficult, but tolerable. To be alone and lonely when giving birth to an unwanted child, though, that memory was more distressingly poignant than any other.

⋆   ⋆   ⋆

'Be a good girl, Janice,' the midwife pleaded, 'it isn't our fault, you know. We're trying to help you.'

'I don't want your bloody help!'

'I think you do, my love, now just do as we ask and you'll be fine.'

'I wish I could get hold of that bastard Sean! I'd give him bloody pregnant! I'd give him labour! Cut his bloody nuts off, I would!'

'Yes, Janice, I know. You're not the first to feel like that, believe me. Now — take some gas and air — come on.'

Janice could smell and taste that mask with its soporific gases. After all this time her senses still remembered.

'It doesn't bloody work!'

'Oh, Janice, you really mustn't throw the equipment around. It does work if you give it a chance. Now, come on, breathe deeply.'

'I can't. I'm in bleeding agony!'

* * *

'Do you want to hold him, Janice?'

'No, take him away.'

'Look at him, though. He's got problems, but he's a lovely little chap.'

'I don't want to hold him.'

'He's going to need you, Janice.'

'No, he's not. He'll need someone, but not me.'

'I'm a social worker, Janice. Now, who is there who might help you with Andrew?'

'Nobody.'

'No mum? Brothers or sisters? Boy-friend?'

'Nobody, I said. I'm on my own — that's the way I like it. I'm not keeping the baby anyway — that's definite — so you needn't try to change my mind. I'd be no good for him . . . I don't want him.'

★   ★   ★

No, there had been no worried husband mopping her forehead — no eager grannies knitting little white clothes — no joy.

Janice put on her stiletto-heeled shoes, her black tights and her skimpiest mini-skirt. Time to go to work.

'A top to show off the cleavage,' she murmured under her breath, 'not that I've got much to show.'

With makeup complete, and cheap, dangly earrings jingling cold against her neck, Janice lit another cigarette and made for Dandy's nightclub. Now, she must forget.

6

Michael Gilchrist waited for Giles in the lobby of Darley Hill Special School. Several other parents were there too, but Michael found himself standing alone, a situation which had become the norm on recent afternoons.

As usual, at the appointed time, doors opened and wheelchairs appeared from all directions. The muffled murmurs of the waiting parents were drowned by the noise of their offspring.

'Hello, Michael,' Mrs. Ballard said cheerily, as she accompanied Giles into the lobby, 'one young man safely delivered.'

'Thank you,' Michael replied, stooping to kiss his son's forehead. 'Have you been a good boy, Giles?'

'He's always a good boy,' Mrs. Ballard put in, as Giles grunted his pleasure at seeing his father. Then, approaching Michael Gilchrist closely, she said in an

114

undertone: 'Are you all right, Michael? You've been looking very tired lately. I've told you before, that some help at home can be arranged. As much as we love these children of ours, we all need a break, you know.'

'No, it isn't Giles . . . but, to tell you the truth, I am a bit worried about something,' Michael confided, relieved to find a sympathetic adult who would listen to him.

'Can I help?' the teacher inquired, guiding Michael over to a quiet corner, whilst the other parents and children gradually left the building.

'I had a visit from a social worker yesterday,' Michael explained, 'it's the first time I've seen one for ages.'

'Well, they do come round occasionally, just one of their unannounced calls, I expect.'

'I don't think so,' Michael argued, shaking his head adamantly. 'I'm pretty sure it's all to do with Joanna's murder.'

'No! Why would it be?'

'Someone told the police that I'd been flirting with Joanna at the Christmas party, and they're trying to make a big thing of it.'

'No . . . really?' Dorothy Ballard's guilt caused her to feel hot and very uncomfortable, but she concealed this admirably.

'They've even dug up some offence from years ago — nothing much, you understand. I was drunk at the time — boys' night out — you know the sort of things that go on.'

'High spirits, of course,' she sympathized.

'Yes, that's all it was, but once you've got a record . . . you know what the police are like.'

'Oh dear.'

'I'm wondering if they contacted the social services about me.'

'No, I shouldn't have thought so.'

'They can think what they like — I've done nothing wrong — but it's Giles. If they convince the social services that I'm unfit to look after him, they might take him away from me.'

Giles watched his friends, happily unaware of his father's words.

'They'd have us to deal with first, Michael. We'd always back you — you're a wonderful father to this boy.'

'It would break Giles's heart if we were separated,' Michael whispered, 'and mine too.'

'I'm sure you're worrying about nothing, Michael, really. It was probably just a routine visit anyway. The sooner this awful murder business is over, the better for everyone.'

'Amen to that.'

'Now, you stop worrying.'

'Mm. It's just that the police seem to have such a poor opinion of me. I felt as though I was a truly evil man by the time they left.'

★ ★ ★

In the murder incident room at Darley New Town Police Station, Silas Blaire and John Skinner sat reading through copious notes and forensic reports. The Chief Inspector put his hands behind his head and leant back in his chair.

'You know, Skinner, Michael Gilchrist

makes me feel as guilty as hell,' he admitted.

'What?' Sergeant Skinner was clearly bewildered.

'Michael Gilchrist . . . you know.'

'Yes, I know who he is, but . . . '

'He's given up everything to look after that boy, hasn't he? Absolutely everything.'

'Well yes, I suppose he has.'

'No suppose about it, Skinner. His job, his social life and his friends too, I shouldn't wonder — all gone so that he can care for his son. It can't be much of a life, can it? Just imagine it. Not even a wife to talk to — bit grim, eh?'

'Yeh, must be.' Sergeant Skinner pondered on his superior officer's words.

'He must be very close to that boy. He's his father and his mother too.'

'Yes, sir, but I don't see why that should make you feel guilty.'

'Don't you, Skinner? It's because I would never have done what Michael Gilchrist has done. I would never have given up my job for James.'

118

'No, but there was no need to, was there, sir?'

'I know, but if there had been the need, I still wouldn't have given up my career to look after my son.'

'Well, everybody's different, it takes all sorts.'

'I had an able-bodied son, Skinner, and I was hardly ever there for him. My job has always taken up too much of my time. Helen used to tell me that, and she was right. When I was with him, I gave him all the wrong messages, that's become obvious. He can't think very much of me at all, can he?'

'I expect he does.' John Skinner was at a loss for words which would reassure.

'No — I drove him away from me and into the arms of my grasping father.'

'That doesn't mean that he doesn't care about you though, sir.'

'Doesn't it, Skinner? I wish I could be sure of that.'

The sergeant felt uncomfortable when Silas spoke of such personal matters, and decided that he should waste no time in steering the Chief Inspector back to the job in hand.

'And what about Joanna Coles, sir?' he asked. 'Michael Gilchrist might be the best father in the world, but do you think he's a murderer? No woman — no sex — obsession with the lovely Mrs. Coles — turned to violence when he was continually rejected — tried to get his thrills that way — what do you think?'

'I think we haven't got enough to go on. We can't point the finger at anyone yet. Whoever it was cleared up after himself too damned well, and don't forget, Skinner, there was no sexual assault.'

'It's unusual to find no skin or particles from clothing under the victim's finger nails too, isn't it?'

'Fairly unusual, yes. I should say he pinned her against the kitchen units with her arms by her sides. The only substances found under her nails were her own blood and the spilt coffee she was lying in. And, of course, the forensic boys have verified that the knife wounds showed the weapon to be a common type — no special dimensions — anyone might

120

own one. It was also scrupulously clean and, therefore, left no traces of any substance in the wounds.'

'And there's no sign of it so far.'

'No — no sign of anything much, Skinner.'

'So we keep on looking then, sir.'

'We do, Skinner. And we say a little prayer too.'

'Mm?'

'We pray that Joanna Coles is his only victim, and not just his first.'

7

Guy found the interior of Dandy's nightclub hot, smoky and depressing. The multi-coloured yet feeble lights twirled with irritating regularity over the dance floor, highlighting the air-born pollution from hundreds of cigarettes. Along one wall was the bar, floodlit and hectic, attracting the thirsty as a magnet attracts pins. On the crowded dance floor, clammy bodies clung to each other; bangled arms were draped around hunched shoulders, while thigh rubbed against thigh.

Guy found this display of wantonness repulsive. To see young men and women so bent on sexual experiment and satisfaction that their self-respect was abandoned, made him sad for humanity. In reality, Guy was a prude. To him, all sex was abhorrent, and he had resolved, in his early teens, that his own body would never be sullied by such a base activity.

He could not bear to think of his mother and father making love. One night, when they had made love, they had made him . . . bastards.

Behind the bar, three men and three women, one of them being Janice Perry, worked frantically. Though there was little time for conversation, Guy could see how the tarty Miss Perry responded with coquettish delight when her male customers, speaking and seeing through an alcoholic haze, flirted with her. The men's familiarity soon revealed to Guy that his next victim was called Janice. He was pleased to know her Christian name.

There was no clemency in Guy's heart as he watched the wretched young woman living her shabby life. Nothing would alter his callous plans. In fact, everything he saw only strengthened his resolve to make Janice Perry his next message to the world.

Standing by the exits, and generally making their presence felt, were several young men of exceptionally large stature. They walked slowly around the club, their barrel chests embellished by the unnatural posture which they all adopted. Guy thought that they looked quite ridiculous as they strutted, with all the self-admiration of the male peacock, but none of the beauty, from one rowdy table to another. Their presence was intended to keep the peace in this ghastly place. Guy thought that a large and effective bomb descending on its heart would be the best thing that could happen to it . . . the misery was now . . . all around him.

Janice, obviously impressed by the size and masculinity of these robust young bodies, advanced on them whenever they approached the bar, enjoying flirtatious repartee and mutual disrespect.

As Guy sat, drinking a shandy and observing his prey, he found it difficult to believe that Janice was a mother. He wondered whether she had done her son a disservice or a favour by almost totally rejecting him. After all, the little boy would not have the overbearing mother to cope with — the woman so bent on compensating for the terrible inheritance she had passed on, that she asphyxiated him with sickly sentimentality, and love born from remorse.

To exclude him from her life, though, was surely an inhuman act, and one which Guy found outrageous and inexcusable . . . no, he decided that she should not have done that. It was as if little Andrew was to blame for his own disabilities, as if Janice had been dissatisfied — even angry — with him; so much so that she needed to deny his very existence.

Guy was pleased with his choice. She would soon be punished.

At ten o'clock, Guy left the nightclub. He had told his mother that he wished to spend an evening in town. As usual, she was relieved to see him back again, and Guy was subjected to the customary questions about his time away from home.

By half past eleven, he was in bed and asleep, but the alarm on his watch was set for one o'clock in the morning. When its timid bleeping sounded, Guy was instantly awake and on his feet. He dressed, and left the house silently, turning off the burglar alarm as he went.

In one of the outhouses, as expected, he found Toby's racing bike. Riding rather shakily, this being his first serious attempt at such a hazardous activity, Guy left Dunbar House and made for Darley New Town.

As he gained in confidence, he was tempted to speed down the lane, to taste freedom and excitement, just for a few minutes. He knew that if he fell, however, his plans would be curtailed, and how would he explain what he was doing on Toby's bike at half past one in the morning? So, very steadily, he rode on towards Dandy's nightclub.

The night was mild, and as he stood on the corner of the street, waiting for first the customers and then the staff to leave the club, a trickle of sweat rolled down Guy's neck. He was thrilled by the thought of another murder.

At two o'clock, the doors of Dandy's club opened, and loud, drunken crowds were discharged onto the pavement. Guy watched as they gradually dispersed, some stumbling, some singing, into the night. It took a little while for the revellers to leave, but the silence which followed their eventual departure was pleasing.

Janice Perry was the first of the staff to appear. It was half past two by now, and Guy was relieved to see his victim at last. Tonight he would find out where she lived, then he could get down to the enjoyable business of planning her death.

Janice pulled her leather jacket tightly around her, put her hands in her pockets and walked briskly along the road, her stiletto heels clinking on the pavements, as though to give advanced warning of her approach. A few yards behind her, Guy followed, pushing his brother's bike and lurking in gloomy shop doorways. Janice seemed completely unaware of Guy's presence. He liked that . . . he had no wish to frighten her . . . not just yet.

As the heedless Miss Perry turned the corner into a narrow and deserted side street, Guy felt sure that she would soon be nearing her home; he hoped so — his hips and knees were becoming painful. He crossed to the opposite side of the road, stopped and watched as she arrived at the grocer's shop above which she lived. She turned her key in the lock of a side door, which lay back in a deep porch to the left of the shop window. Janice Perry was safely at home.

Guy cycled slowly back to Dunbar House, returned Toby's bike to its usual resting-place and went indoors. He switched the burglar alarms on, and was soon back in bed, aching and drained, but extremely satisfied with his night's work.

8

Jean Barnett stretched her legs and wiggled her toes in front of the fake log fire, which warmed her lounge.

'It's been pure hell in that office today,' she moaned to her husband. 'If they don't soon replace Joanna with somebody who's in possession of a brain, I'll go mad. This youngster I've got with me at the moment is worse than useless.'

'Oh dear,' Peter sympathized absently, clearly not interested in his wife's predicament.

'You seem a bit elsewhere tonight, what's wrong?' Jean asked, agitated by Peter's indifference.

'Jean . . . '

'Yes?'

'Jean, I've got to tell you something.'

'Well go on then — we've never had secrets, have we? What is it?'

'It isn't easy, Jean. I had hoped you wouldn't need to know, but the way things are going, I'm afraid you'll find out from the newspapers or the police or some gossip who's in the know, and that would be so much worse.'

'The newspapers? What are you talking about, Peter?'

'It's about Joanna.'

'Joanna?'

'Yes, I'm afraid so. When the police were searching her house, they found a letter.' Peter paused and turned away from his wife.

'So?'

'It was a letter from me.'

'From you to Joanna?' Jean stood up and forced Peter to face her again.

'I wrote her a note, Jean,' he admitted with uneasy vigour. 'That's all — I was drunk and, on the spur of the moment, I wrote to her.'

'I don't need to ask what the letter was about,' Jean said, condemnation and sorrow struggling for supremacy in her heart and her eyes. 'The guilt in your face leaves me in no doubt whatsoever . . . you wanted to have an affair with her, didn't you?'

'I asked her to meet me in secret . . .'

'Yes! So that you could take her to bed — that's what you wanted, isn't it?'

'I suppose so — I don't really know what I wanted.'

'Oh give me credit for some intelligence, Peter, please. You wanted sex with Joanna,'

Peter tried to placate his wife, whose venomous temper he had grown to know well over the years.

'Absolutely nothing happened, Jean,' he assured her, placing his hands gently on her shoulders.

'Why should I believe you?'

'Honestly — we never met — not just the two of us — not once!'

'Get cold feet, did you?'

'I posted the letter while I was still under the influence of too many glasses of wine and two or three brandies. Once I'd sobered up and realized what I'd done, I regretted it — I really did.'

'You still wanted her, though, didn't you? It's just that when you were drunk, you had the guts to let your real feelings guide your actions, instead of keeping them restrained behind your bloody

131

hypocritical decency!'

'No, Jean!'

'Why can't you at least be honest and tell me that you wanted to make love to her? Why do you have to hide behind the effects of alcohol? You didn't suddenly fancy her when you'd had a few drinks — you'd wanted her since you first saw her, hadn't you? I used to see the way you stared at her.'

'Nothing happened, Jean!'

'That isn't the point, Peter. The point is that you wanted to make love to her — that's what counts.'

'Oh, come on . . . I thought she was attractive — yes — haven't you ever looked at another man and . . .'

'Wanted to go to bed with him?' Jean put in, her face growing wild and vivacious as her eyes widened. 'No — no, as a matter of fact, I haven't!'

'Look, I do think you're over-reacting just a little,' Peter suggested meekly, as though he did not believe his own words.

'Oh, do you — do you really?'

'Nothing happened! We didn't even meet!'

'Spur of the moment thing!' Jean mocked. 'The truth of it is, that the booze just nullified your conscience! You wanted to have sex with her and you'd wanted to for months!'

'Jean, please.'

'Did she answer your letter?'

'No.'

'She just ignored it?'

'Not exactly.'

'Well, what then?'

'She came to see me at the office one day.'

'So, you did meet then?'

'No — not like that. Joanna came to the office to tell me that she realized the letter was a mistake — that she knew I'd be regretting the fact that I'd ever sent it. She said that she loved Stuart and she knew that I loved you.'

'So, you were sent packing like a randy dog, who's sniffing round a bitch on heat. And what would have happened if she'd said, 'O.K., Peter, I'm game if you are' — mm? You'd have jumped for joy and booked a hotel room, wouldn't you? Wouldn't you?'

133

Jean was becoming hysterical.

'Calm down now,' Peter pleaded. 'You really mustn't get yourself in such a state, Jean.'

'Oh, mustn't I? I'm so sorry, Peter. It's just that I've found I don't really know the man I've been married to for all these years. I thought I did, but I don't! Now, answer me please truthfully. If Joanna had accepted your proposition, you'd have had an affair with her, wouldn't you? Tell me!'

'No — probably not!' Peter's head was bowed and his eyes avoided his wife's questioning stare.

'Probably not! You must think I'm bloody stupid! You'd have been in bed with her the first chance you had!'

'But nothing did happen — surely that's the main thing.'

'Do you know, Peter, I almost wish you had slept with her!'

'What?' Peter was totally baffled by his wife's words.

'You'd have looked less like a naughty little boy who got his wrists slapped!'

'I don't . . . '

'It's humiliating to think that the woman you fancied sent you away and told you not to be so silly. I feel humiliated for you and for myself!'

'I don't understand you, Jean. Please, let's just stop all this right now. I love you and I always have done. I didn't love Joanna and I never made love to her. Let's get all this into perspective, shall we?'

'I can't just forget it, Peter. I would have trusted you with anyone, I really would. How wrong can you be? I'll never be able to trust you again, you realize that, don't you? I feel deceived and I feel stupid for not seeing the way things were going. How can I respect you now? Fancying a woman, far younger than you are, to the point where you make yourself look a pathetic, middle-aged fool over her. No, Peter, I'll never feel the same way about you again.' Jean turned away from her subdued and contrite husband. 'I'm going out,' she announced, feverishly changing into her outdoor shoes. 'I don't know what time I'll be back, but I won't disturb you. I'll be sleeping in the spare room.'

9

In a warm, cosy tea-shop in Darley New Town, Alex Dunbar and her friend Kate sat chatting, whilst indulging their passion for cream cakes and piping hot earl grey. This had always been a favourite ritual of theirs after a heavy afternoon's shopping.

'Damn!' Alex exclaimed suddenly.

'What?' Kate inquired, wiping cream from her upper lip with her napkin in as ladylike a manner as was possible.

'I came straight past the ironmonger's — my memory is getting worse by the minute — I'm sure it is.'

'What did you want then? We can go back — it isn't far.'

'Mm, I suppose so. My best kitchen knife has vanished; I know where it went. Mrs. O'Brian has thrown it out with the vegetable peelings — she's done it before.'

'Has she?' Kate chuckled.

'Yes, she's a dear, of course, but she is a little bit careless sometimes.'

The two friends finished their refreshments and then walked back along the main street towards the ironmonger's.

'When I was talking to Guy last week,' Kate began tentatively, 'he was saying how much he'd like to pass his driving test and get a car.'

'Was he now?'

'Mm.'

'You don't fool me for one minute, Kate,' Alex scolded, a grin softening her face. 'Guy's got at you, hasn't he? He's told you to try and get round me over this blasted car business.'

'No — not at all!'

'Liar!'

The two women laughed.

'Well, all right then, he has, but I can see his point, Alex, I really can. The boy's getting very depressed about the wheelchair, you know. He has to use it much more than he did. A car would give him such a lot of independence and freedom.'

'I know, but . . . '

'And may I remind you, my love, that if

Guy wants to get a car and learn to drive it, there's absolutely nothing you can do to stop him.'

'Yes, Kate, but he knows that the very idea of his learning to drive terrifies me. I'd never have a minute's peace while he was out in the damned car. Guy wouldn't put me through that sort of anxiety.'

'Toby has a sports car.'

'Yes, and he's pranged it twice! He had a terrible bump on his forehead the second time — now, if that had been Guy . . . '

'I know, Alex, but you can't wrap him up in cotton wool for the rest of his life.'

'I can try.'

'Alex!'

'You know what young men are like in cars, Kate. He'd be putting his foot down like all the others do.'

'I think you're underestimating Guy's common sense. He only wants a car to get him from A to B; he isn't going to use the roads as a racetrack. I'm sure he'd be careful. Guy doesn't want to injure himself any more than you want him to, does he?'

'I don't know,' Alex replied, her face suddenly becoming sombre and pensive.

'What do you mean? Of course he doesn't want to get hurt.'

'Guy frightens me sometimes, Kate . . . terrifies me, in fact. I look at him and I see a side to his nature that I don't really know . . . a dark side, if you like.' Alex was near to tears.

'Oh come on, love,' Kate cajoled, 'he's a bit thoughtful sometimes, I know, but who isn't? You just take more notice of his moods than anyone else's because it's Guy and he has special problems. We all have our quieter side, Alex — you must allow Guy to have his too.'

'No, it isn't just his moods, Kate. It's his attitude to life — to his own life. I sometimes think that he doesn't care about his own safety — his own survival. I don't think he would be careful in a car — I think he would take stupid risks and to hell with the consequences. I don't believe that his own life is particularly important to him.'

'You're imagining it, Alex, I'm sure you are. He probably doesn't fuss about himself as much as you fuss about him, but he still values his life.'

'I do hope so, Kate. I've been seeing his dark side more and more recently and it's alarming. I so want what's best for him . . . that's all I've ever wanted.'

'I know, Alex.' Kate nudged her friend's arm. 'Hey, the ironmonger's — here we are — kitchen knife — remember?'

★ ★ ★

At two o'clock the following morning, while his mother and his Aunt Kate slept soundly in their respective homes, Guy Dunbar stood amid the shadows outside Dandy's nightclub.

Once again he had borrowed Toby's racing bike, once again his gloved hands gripped the handlebars, but this time, hidden in the saddlebag, was the lost kitchen knife.

Tonight, Guy would murder Janice Perry.

It seemed an agonizing age before the disorderly clientele of Dandy's nightclub melted into the darkness and the street fell silent. Soon she would be there, unaware of her imminent fate, and Guy was waiting — all-powerful and capable of anything — absolutely anything. He must savour this strength . . . it gave his life purpose and great pleasure.

When Janice Perry emerged from the club, Guy's annoyance at what he saw was so acute that he almost screamed his fury at her. She was not alone. He watched in near horror as she walked along the path with one of the other barmaids.

Quickly calming himself, Guy decided to follow them anyway, hoping that the other woman would not go all the way to Janice's flat with her.

He walked stealthily, several yards behind them, his trainers making no sound on the dry pavements. The voices of the young women, shrill and vulgar, encroached on the night's natural quietness. Guy hated them both.

As he followed, keeping himself and Toby's bicycle against the walls of the ugly buildings, Guy's knees and ankles grew painful. He needed to stop and rest, but determination forced him to go on. At the corner of the street before Janice Perry's turning, her friend left her, entering one of the terraced houses, which typified this part of Darley New Town. Guy was relieved; at last he could do his work.

Now that she was alone, Janice's pace quickened, and so, therefore, did Guy's. The increased speed, however, caused increased bruising to his joints and his suffering narrowed his handsome eyes and made them water, though no one was present to witness it.

He longed to be there, outside the grocer's shop, in that deep, dark porch, but the pain was becoming unbearable. Suddenly, his left leg gave way under him, causing him to stumble against the bicycle, which in turn clattered noisily into a telegraph pole. Janice Perry turned and saw him behind her. She seemed instinctively to know of his intent, because her fast walk became an unsteady trot. Guy tried to mount the cycle, but his knees would not bend, nor would his legs be lifted to the necessary height.

Janice glanced behind her again. Her

heartbeat quickened, and her congested, smoke-stained lungs became bellows, working more frantically with each uncertain clink of those spindly heels on the pavement. She panted her foul breath out into the night air, her mouth open and fish-like. The sound of the pulses inside her skull grew thunderous, like the hard, rhythmic vibration of a bass drum. Janice felt sick with fear. Her tight skirt would not allow her to lengthen her stride, so her bony legs moved with ungainly speed, but little efficiency, towards her home.

Guy stumbled, as quickly as he was able, along the path behind her, but the gap between them was growing longer. The grocer's shop was only a few yards away now, and he cried out in stark frustration as he realized that he could not catch her.

Watching the terrified Janice disappear into the porch and hearing the front door slam behind her, afforded Guy such despair that he fell, momentarily to his knees, hanging his head like a disappointed child. He knew that he must get up, though, and get away from this place. There was no way that he could ride Toby's bicycle back to Dunbar House until he had rested his legs and taken some drugs which would bring him a little relief. He struggled to his feet and crept back along the dark street. Leaning on the cycle for support, he made for Darley New Town Railway Station, which was only a couple of minutes away.

Three or four people lay on the bench-seats in the station, possibly awaiting the first train of the next day, but more than likely homeless, and enjoying the relative shelter of the dimly lit building. Guy propped the bike against the wall of the station and found himself an empty bench on which to lie. He swallowed the tablets which would ease his distress. They stuck momentarily in his dry throat. After setting the alarm on his watch for half past four, he attempted to rest his painful legs and hips.

The alarm was, in the event, unnecessary. Guy's body may have been still, but his mind was fiercely active. He could not close his eyes, let alone sleep.

As he thought back over the night's events, Guy's resentment of his ailing body was more harrowing than his physical pain. His frustration was acute; he had failed in his mission. He knew only too well that he would soon need his wheelchair all the time, but his absolute resolution to do his work would not allow him to give in to such a restricted lifestyle yet . . . he had not finished. He must not let his mind become captive in his defective body; his thoughts must remain free and strong and in control of his actions.

Next time he would succeed.

At half past four, Guy began his journey back to Dunbar House. By now, the drugs were working, and the pain in his joints was not as excruciating as it had been, though he had never before felt so relieved to get into his bed. Though anger at his failure still smouldered inside him, sheer exhaustion caused Guy to sleep. The knife, meant for murder, lay waiting, wrapped in a small towel and hidden, with a purpose bought plastic mackintosh in one of his cupboards . . . its day would soon come.

In the morning, Guy's determination to succeed in killing Janice Perry was overwhelming. It was the only thing that seemed real to him. His vexation, when he thought of his aborted attempt to murder this young woman, had abated now, superseded by the barbarous will-power which drove him relentlessly on to kill again. He felt as though he was looking at his surroundings through borrowed eyes. The world was indistinct and unimportant, and his family so very unaware. His message to humanity was his only concern, and Janice Perry would be part of that message before very long.

★ ★ ★

'You look worn out, Guy,' Alex remarked, as she shared a late breakfast with him, 'didn't you sleep properly?'

'No — not really — bad dreams, you know.'

'What were they about, darling?'

'Oh, nothing specific — just a load of rubbish all jumbled up.'

146

'Why don't you go back to bed for a while?'

'No, there's no need.'

'You're not sitting where I am, Guy Dunbar! I'd say there was definitely a need.'

'Well, perhaps I'll have a nap later — don't fuss, Mother.'

'Aunt Kate was telling me about your wanting to learn to drive,' Alex said, after a pause in the conversation. 'I mean, I've always known you wanted to learn, but she said that you feel more strongly about it now — is that right?'

'Yes, I suppose it is,' Guy answered, trying to keep his mind on the here and now.

'Well, I've had a wonderful idea,' Alex enthused.

'Oh, what's that?'

'I'm going to get you your own car and a chauffeur to go with it.'

'What?' Guy was suddenly very much in the present.

'Yes — he'll be yours to command. When you don't want him, he can look after the upkeep of all the vehicles. It would suit a retired policeman — somebody with an advanced driving licence.'

'I don't want a chauffeur!'

'No problem, Guy — your father and I can afford it. Your birthday's coming up — call it a birthday present.'

'I'm not worried about the money, Mother! I'm telling you that I don't want a bloody chauffeur!'

'But it's the ideal solution.'

'Who for? It must be you — it certainly isn't for me!' Guy wanted to smash everything on the breakfast table. He almost did. Restraint was difficult to muster on this particular morning. 'You just don't understand, do you, Mother?' His exasperation was impossible to contain. He brought his clenched fist down on the table.

'You'll hurt yourself, Guy!' Alex half cried. 'I don't think you should be angry when I've only your interests at heart!'

'Really? Don't you? Maybe you're right, but I think that it must be your interests that you really have in your heart!'

'No, Guy. I only want what's best for

you, darling. You know that!'

'You don't want me driving my own car, and this is one way round the problem. You're not thinking of me!'

'I am, Guy! I would feel happier if an experienced driver took you around — yes — but my main concern is that I want to give you more independence and mobility. I do understand how you feel, darling, believe me, please. It's just that I'm terrified of you getting hurt.' Alex sobbed, her eyes pleading with her son not to make her live through all that fear. 'You know that I'd never do anything to upset you, Guy. I so want you to have a good, contented life . . . nothing else really matters to me. You're so very special, darling . . . so very special.'

'I know, Mother.' Guy was ostensibly calm; he knew that he must be. As he walked to her side and took her in his arms, however, he so needed to hurt her — to kill her. 'I'm sorry,' he whispered, 'I'll have your chauffeur, if that's what you want.'

'It'll be best,' Alex murmured, kissing her son's cheek and embracing him as a lover might have done.

'Yes, of course it will. I'll get used to the idea, no doubt. Give me time. You're right, as usual.'

'I love you, Guy.'

'And I love you, Mother.'

Guy wished, with all his heart, that his words told a lie, but they did not.

★ ★ ★

That afternoon, when Guy was taking the rest which Alex had insisted he needed, he felt more bitterly dissatisfied with his life than usual.

His plans for Janice Perry gave him a purpose. That was good, but was it enough? He must not become the common killer — hated and never understood. The world must know the truth. Everyone must realize that he had been chosen to tell that truth. In time, he would be revered, if he could just get it right. Yes, there was a way.

Now, at last, Guy knew what he must do. A nebulous idea, which he had buried in the dormant recesses of his mind, emerged to confront him with persuasive inevitability. He must murder his own mother. Alex would be his final victim . . . then the world would understand. The execution of his mother would be the climax — the final spectacle. Then he would have peace.

Although he loved her, Guy knew that Alex deserved to die. He had no doubts at all about that. And to rid humanity of her altruistic sentimentality would be a fitting culmination to his work. He would no longer simply wish to kill her one hundred times a day, no, he would do it. He would really do it. Guy was certain that he would know when her time had come.

Yes, his own mother must die. He would find fulfilment in her death — what justice!

10

'How much longer do we have to wait before we can organize Joanna's funeral?' Stuart Coles asked Chief Inspector Blaire in the business-like atmosphere of the incident room at Darley New Town Police Station. 'I can't go on for much longer with things as they are.'

'It's always a strain for families in such cases, Mr. Coles. I do sympathize, but when it's murder, I'm afraid the body cannot be released for burial immediately. These things take time.'

'I can't sleep at night.' Stuart gulped air loudly, in an attempt not to cry. 'I just lie in bed thinking of her on some cold slab in a huge refrigerator, and I want to hold her so much . . . to let her know that she's not alone . . . that I haven't deserted her. God, that sounds so bloody stupid when I put it into words.'

'No, Mr. Coles — no, it doesn't.'

'It's as though she's imprisoned —

being punished — instead of the bastard that murdered her.'

Silas Blaire closed the file that lay on his desk before him. It seemed inappropriate to use notes from a numbered case record when talking to the murdered woman's husband. He wanted Stuart to understand that he cared about Joanna's death — that he thought of her as a person and not simply a crime to be solved.

'We're doing all we can to find the killer, Mr. Coles,' he said gently. 'You haven't thought of anyone from your wife's past who may have borne a grudge, I suppose.'

'No — no, I haven't.' Stuart tried to summon all his anger, he found it therapeutic in dealing with his sorrow. 'What about the weapon — has that been found?'

'No, I'm afraid not. But, as the murderer had clearly planned the crime, he had no doubt decided in advance how to dispose of the weapon too.'

'I still can't believe that somebody actually sat down and methodically devised a plan to murder Joanna —

someone who knew her too — or she would never have undone that chain lock.' Stuart Coles shook his head, the burden of his torment dragging down his features, so that he looked far older than his years. 'I mean, why? She was so good — so perfect.'

'Yes. I don't mind telling you that motive is one huge stumbling block for us at the moment. We're clutching at straws in that department.'

'What straws?'

'Mm?'

'Well, that suggests that you've got some ideas — something to go on — is that right?'

'Not anything of any substance, Mr. Coles. We've no real evidence against anyone as yet.'

'No, but you've one or two names in your mind, haven't you?'

'No, we've nothing substantial to go on at all — please don't read anything into my words.'

'You would tell me, Chief Inspector, wouldn't you?'

'When we have anything concrete, yes,

I will keep you informed, Mr. Coles, I promise you that.'

'I want someone to blame, you see — someone other than myself.'

'Yourself?'

'Yes, if I hadn't left her that evening for a bloody game of squash!'

'Mr. Coles, don't punish yourself. It won't help. It wasn't your fault.'

'I feel guilty, though, so terribly guilty — and useless too. Can't I do anything to help you people — I need to help.'

'Er . . . I did want to ask you something . . . something rather delicate, I'm afraid.'

'Go ahead, Chief Inspector.'

'Do you know of anyone — any men — who might have . . . '

'Fancied Joanna?'

'Well, yes.'

'Any number of men, I should think. She was very beautiful.'

'Yes, but had anybody — made advances of any kind? Were you aware of anyone bothering her at all?'

'No. Oh, except for poor old Peter — Peter Barnett. He wrote her a letter a while back.'

'Yes, we found it.'

'I wouldn't call that bothering her, though. I mean, that was nothing. Joanna and I had quite a chuckle about it when she showed me the note. She called into his office and put him in his place — gently, of course. If Jean had found out, she would have killed him . . . Christ, what am I saying?' Stuart closed his eyes as if to rid his mind of those reckless words. 'I mean . . . I mean that Jean would have lost her temper; she's a bit vitriolic, is Jean.'

'So, you attached absolutely no importance to the letter from Mr. Barnett?'

'Good God, no. It was all a bit pathetic really. We both felt sorry for Peter. He didn't know that Joanna had shown me the note, but I could see how embarrassed he was, when he and Jean came round to visit.'

'You weren't jealous at all?'

'No.' Stuart looked momentarily uneasy. 'No — there was nothing to be jealous about. Joanna was completely honest with me and faithful too. I know that. If you trust your partner, then there's no need

156

for jealousy, is there? You feel rather proud to know that other men find your wife attractive, and, as long as it's all one-sided, it's somehow flattering too — because she only wants you. Do you understand what I mean?'

'Yes, I do.'

'If I'd thought that anyone was really pestering Joanna, then I would have done something about it. I'd have shown no mercy. But Peter's note . . . no, I think you can forget that one, Chief Inspector Blaire.'

'Yes, I see. Thank you, Mr. Coles.'

★   ★   ★

The police, floundering in their tunnel of unfounded suspicions, were coming no nearer to identifying the murderer of Joanna Coles. They could not be blamed for their ignorance of the truth. Why should they link the name of this killer to his victim? To attain such enlightenment, they would need to penetrate one very sick and labyrinthine mind.

157

11

Guy had decided to wait until his limbs had fully recovered from his first attempt on Janice Perry's life, before trying again. There must be no more failure — no more agonizing frustration. A time lapse would also restore Janice's confidence about walking home alone. She was bound to be more wary than usual after being followed. Yes, he must give her fear time to subside. Anyway, there was great pleasure to be gained from the anticipation of her murder. He would satisfy himself with that for now, and an occasional visit to Dandy's club, of course, where he could savour the unawareness of his next victim.

'Come here, Guy!' Alex's voice preceded her as she hurried, with crimson face, into Guy's sitting room.

'What is it, Mother?'

'Just come with me — it's good news!' She took Guy's hand and led him to the drawing room, where Toby, Phillip and a young woman awaited his arrival. 'Tell your brother then, Toby,' Alex urged, seeming far more animated by her excitement than Guy had seen her for a long time.

'This is Tessa,' Toby announced proudly to Guy, 'my fiancée.'

The tall, slim young woman stepped forward and took Guy's hand. She had an abundance of fair hair, which hung loosely curled around her shoulders, and her eyes were the palest, most delicate blue. Tessa epitomized femininity.

Guy was quite taken aback when she pressed her full, pink lips against his cheek.

'It'll be great to have a brother-in-law,' she whispered, as though the two of them were alone in the room. 'I'm an only child, and you don't know how pleased I am that Toby isn't. We'll be good friends, won't we?'

'Yes, of course,' Guy answered, charmed by this vivacious young woman.

'Mm, not too friendly though, eh?' Toby joked, taking Tessa's hand from Guy.

After the time honoured congratulations and a toast in Phillip's best champagne, the Dunbar family and Tessa Gregg sat down to dinner. Everything seemed congenial, even loving, but that was because no one present could tap into Guy's thoughts.

While plans for the wedding were discussed, he sat eating, with more enthusiasm than usual, to avoid being drawn into the futile conversation which both surrounded and infuriated him.

'You'll be my best man, won't you, Guy?' Toby asked so earnestly that the only course of action open to Guy was to agree and appear pleased to be given such a doubtful honour.

By the time the main course was finished, Guy had completely retreated into his private and introspective hell. Alex could see that he did not want to contribute to the discussion concerning the coming celebrations, and she surmised that envy was the root of his self-inflicted isolation.

In fact, Guy was contemplating whether or not he should murder Tessa Gregg.

It would have to be before Alex — yes — the one before his mother. Janice Perry next, then Tessa and then Alex.

Guy was not enjoying this deadly deliberation; it was less straightforward than it should be. He was used to conflict in his mind. It was so familiar to him that it was curiously comforting. This present dilemma, however, caused his thoughts to become ensnared in a mesh of compulsion and confusion. His head was alive with pain.

Guy's present perplexity was largely due to an alien feeling, a sensation which distressed him, and one which he knew he must repress and control. He was being confronted with the ability to care — to really care, and, at this time, he could not cope with it.

Toby was the problem. The two brothers had always been very good friends. Guy was a little surprised that Toby had not mentioned his forthcoming engagement to him, but there had always been a secretive side to the youngest Mr. Dunbar. This marriage business was such a shock, though, such a disaster. Guy sipped his coffee and stared at Tessa, who was giving forth on the subject of wedding cakes — size, shape, decorations and the like. If he were to murder her, Guy pondered, Toby would suffer. It was impossible for Guy to empathize with that kind of suffering. It was utterly unknown to him — an emotion only for others — but he did know that such pain existed.

What was of such grave concern to Guy now, was that he cared about Toby's feelings, and caring was obstructive to his work. What if he let Tessa live though? There would be the ridiculous, ritualistic wedding and then the sex. Before too long, the babies would come, and Tessa would be a mother, but a mother to what? No . . . Guy could not allow that. He would have to act.

'I've got a headache,' he said suddenly, interrupting talk of bridesmaids and taffeta.

'Oh, Guy,' Alex whined, 'what a shame. Have a lie down, darling. I'll come and give you your injection in a minute.'

'Can I watch?' Tessa asked, as though

her favourite programme was about to come on the television.

'What?' Guy demanded, once more surprised by the actions of Toby's intended.

'I've just started training as a nurse, Guy,' Tessa explained, 'didn't you know?'

'Er, no, I didn't.'

'We haven't done injections yet, but if you don't mind, I'd love to watch your mother give you your factor eight.'

'No, no, I don't mind.' Guy smiled weakly, as Tessa nodded, clearly relishing the thought of the joy to come.

'You'll have to tell me all about your illness one day,' Tessa said, while Alex prepared to give Guy his injection.

'It isn't an illness, it's a condition.' Guy corrected the eager Tessa kindly.

'Oh, I'm so sorry. Put that down to ignorance, Guy, won't you? I haven't offended you, have I?'

'No, no, not at all.'

'I so want to be a good nurse. I'll have to learn not to put my foot in it, won't I?'

'You'll be a splendid nurse,' Alex reassured, 'I know that because you're so eager to succeed, and that's half the battle.'

Tessa watched, enthralled, as Alex administered the syringe full of liquid, which made Guy's life just about endurable.

'Don't worry, Guy,' Tessa laughed, her eyes glinting with gentle mischief, 'I won't practise on you!'

Guy grinned; he liked Tessa. What a shame he would have to murder her.

★　★　★

That night, sleep did not come easily to Guy. He tried to imagine Toby and Tessa having sex. It was as though he needed to see this evil act in his mind's eye; it would strengthen his resolve to complete his mission. Guy rarely used the term making love; he found it risible. It was all sex after all; there was no difference. Why did people believe that a church wedding, with all the paraphernalia, could somehow sanitize the act of sex? And what was love? A label given to carnal desire in man, which made it somehow acceptable

164

to people who could not bear to admit that they were simply animals acting on their basest instincts.

Guy considered the extinction of the human species to be a desirable event — and the sooner the better.

The image of Toby pounding himself into Tessa's receptive body expelled all former doubts from Guy's mind. The vision was vile, and no mawkish misgivings must be allowed to interfere with what he knew was the right thing to do.

* * *

About a week after the engagement, Aunt Kate sat with Guy in the kitchen of Dunbar House.

'Tessa seems a very pleasant girl, don't you think?' she asked. 'A sanguine personality, I'd say. She and Toby should make a grand couple.'

'Yes, they should. She's . . . very friendly.'

'Where did you say your mother had gone?'

'She's at the dressmaker's with Tessa

— choosing a pattern or something.'

'You're a typical man, young Guy. You couldn't be less interested in the big day, could you?'

Guy smiled at his favourite aunt.

'Is it that obvious?'

'I'm afraid it is. Oh, it's all right with me, but make sure you enter into the spirit of things with your mother and Toby, or they might feel a bit hurt.'

'Yes, you're quite right. It's just that weddings aren't my cup of tea.'

'No — mine neither!'

'Really?'

'Mm . . . I hate the things. I suppose it's because I've never had one of my own — jealousy perhaps — I don't know.'

'I've never thought about that,' Guy answered with pensive compassion, 'you've always just been there, as you are, our Aunt Kate. I've never considered the possibility that you could have married.'

'No, I don't suppose you have, Guy.' Aunt Kate leaned across the kitchen table and squeezed her Godson's hand. 'I only ever loved one man,' she explained, her eyes willing Guy to receive the message beneath her words, 'and he married someone else — a dear friend of mine — so that was that.'

'Oh, Aunt Kate,' Guy had understood the secret confession, which she had never before conveyed to another living soul, and he felt closer to her than he ever had, because she had confided in him.

'Don't you pity me, my love,' she said, 'it's all ancient history now — quite a few gallons have flowed under that famous bridge since then.' She let go of Guy's hand and took a deep breath, as though her spirit was lighter. 'They're not wasting much time, are they, Toby and Tessa?' she went on. 'I mean, the first Saturday in April. It won't be long, will it?'

'No, they do seem in a bit of a hurry.'

'Still — why not? When I was a girl, my father would have considered it to be unseemly haste, but things are so different now.'

Guy was still fascinated by his aunt's veiled revelation. He was regretting desperately the fact that his father had not chosen Aunt Kate for his wife, and left Alex to remain a spinster. Aunt Kate would not have passed on that nefarious gene to him. It was all so cruel — so unjust — that he should know such suffering because of other people's actions.

'Good God it's nearly lunchtime,' he remarked, leaving his intimate anger to ferment like a fine wine approaching its peak. 'Where the hell have they got to?'

'It's bound to take a while, Guy.'

'I wish Tessa had a mother, then she could do all this arranging and organizing: dresses, cakes, flowers, cars, guest-lists and everything else. Mother's never at home.'

'I expect Alex is enjoying every minute of it.'

'Maybe. Do you know, she almost forgot to pick up my prescription yesterday. Can you imagine that? Mother forgetting my prescription!'

'I should say that's a positive sign. I mean, you've always wanted her to let go a bit, haven't you? It's good that she's got so involved in all the preparations.'

'All she talks about is Toby and Tess

and the bloody wedding!'

'Guy — I do believe you're jealous!'

'Jealous — no way!'

'Yes, you are. You've always hated the way your mother fusses over you, the way she's devoted her life to you. You've told me yourself that her obsession with your wellbeing has suffocated you, but now that she's all involved with Toby and the wedding, you don't like it. You're feeling cheated — left out — it's perfectly natural.'

'I'm not, Aunt Kate.'

'I've never pussy-footed around you, my love, and I won't start now. You're jealous of Toby and your mother for the first time in your life, but once he's married, she'll be back to normal. You'll have her to yourself.'

'See you later, Aunt Kate,' Guy snarled, leaving the kitchen with surly speed.

The deserted woman smiled to herself.

'Yes, the truth hurts, doesn't it, young Guy?' she murmured to his empty chair.

A few seconds later, Guy stood in the drawing room, spitting obscenities at the serene luxury which surrounded him.

169

He turned to his mother's bureau and snatched up a huge pile of wedding invitations. Alex had spent all the previous evening writing on and then addressing the dainty silver and white cards. Guy, with much satisfaction, threw them onto the log fire, which burned fiercely in the grate.

'That should cause some annoyance and confusion,' he mused, as the final few invitations turned into charred and curling ashes. He took two large logs from the log-box, lay them on top of the evidence, and then went to his rooms, where welcome solitude would be his.

Guy sat in his favourite armchair deliberating on his plans. He would go to Dandy's club and dispose of Janice Perry the following night. He was well rested now and, this time, he would leave the club before she did, so that he could cycle slowly to her street and wait there for her. In this way, he would not have the pleasure of following her, but he would not fail because of the pain in his overtired limbs either. And, after all, the enjoyment would still be his in that porch

— that deep, dark porch. Yes, she would have her terror then . . . it was all so right — so just.

Tessa, of course, would be more difficult. She was almost one of the family — very close to home. He would have to work on the secret demise of Tessa Gregg.

After his mother's death, he would want to explain, to those who did not understand, the purpose behind his actions — his cause. Such careful planning, therefore, would not be necessary. He would be proud to boast to the world about Alex's execution, but he must not be stopped after Tessa's death. She was not the final climax; he must maintain his freedom until his work was completed.

Guy reminded himself that Janice Perry must have priority until he had rid the world of her. It seemed an age since Joanna Coles, but now it was just a few more hours and Janice's punishment would be delivered. Excitement flooded Guy's odious mind; he felt like a small child on Christmas Eve.

171

★　★　★

When the following night arrived, Guy found Dandy's nightclub as loud and depressing as ever. He went to the bar to get a drink, but to his horror, saw that Janice Perry was not working there. He composed himself quickly, ordered a shandy and then said nonchalantly to the young man who served him:

'You're busy tonight — you look run off your feet. Are you short-staffed?'

'We are, yes. One of the girls is in hospital — slipped disc or something — she's in traction. Can't stop — have a good evening!'

'Yes — thanks.'

Guy was mortified. He took a few gulps of his drink and then left the club. It was one o'clock in the morning; he detested the world and everyone in it. As he cycled slowly back to Dunbar House, a light rain began to fall. The drops from heaven camouflaged the tears on his face. His despair was so profound that he was scarcely aware of the narrow, unlit lane, which stretched before him. He moved with mechanical apathy until he reached Dunbar House. He had no energy left for anger — misery was far less exhausting.

That night, Guy slept because he could not bear to be awake. To be conscious was to feel a raw and biting anguish, and he had no strength for that.

The following morning found Guy trying to postpone the new day. He buried his head under the bedclothes in an attempt to stay in his dark, warm cocoon.

It was when he was in that pleasing state between sleeping and waking, when all reality is muffled, that he remembered.

★ ★ ★

Guy was about eight years old and Toby only five or six. The two of them were hiding under Guy's bedclothes, giggling and making plans for a midnight feast.

When they were certain that everyone had gone to bed, the small boys crept down the main stairs of Dunbar House and into the kitchen, where the warmth of the day still lingered.

'Where are those biscuits with the creamy stuff in?' Toby asked.

'They're in this tin,' Guy replied knowledgeably. 'I'll get them — you make some sandwiches — do chocolate spread.'

Toby began to do his brother's bidding. The children were delighted by their prank, and being up in the middle of the night made it all so exciting, when suddenly:

'Ouch!' Toby squealed. 'Ouch — I've cut my hand on that stupid knife! Guy — it hurts!'

'Don't cry, Toby,' Guy begged. 'You'll wake Mummy and Daddy — please don't cry.'

'No, I won't,' Toby whimpered, biting his bottom lip, a habit which he still retained in situations where the utmost restraint was required.

'Let me see.'

Guy took Toby's injured hand.

'Look, there's blood all over the butter,' the wounded one exclaimed.

'Oh don't worry about that, Toby. Mummy will wash it.' Guy picked up the offending knife, which, being meant for

174

fruit, had a sharp point. He gave it to his brother. 'Cut me, Toby!' he commanded. 'Cut my hand too.'

'No — you mustn't get cut, Guy!'

'Just do as I say and cut my hand, Toby!'

'No, I won't. Mummy told me — you've got funny blood and you mustn't ever get cut — not even a little bit!'

'Give me the knife and I'll do it myself then,'

'Why?' Toby demanded, hiding the knife behind his back. 'Why do you want to cut yourself? It's silly!'

'Because if I make my blood mix with yours, then I might catch your good blood.'

'Might you?'

'Yes, and then my blood would be healthy like yours, and I wouldn't need injections all the time, and I could come to school with you, and go to parties and go horse-riding and everything!'

'Ask mummy first!'

'There's no time, you'll stop bleeding in a minute.'

Guy snatched the knife from Toby's trembling fingers, and, showing quite remarkable courage, brought it down hard into the palm of his right hand.

'Your blood looks the same as mine,' Toby commented, confusion aiding his recovery.

'Never mind that. Quick, give me your hand. Let me mix our blood, Toby, so that I can catch your good blood and not be like I am any more!'

Guy pressed the palm of his hand on Toby's and rubbed hard.

'You're bleeding too much!' Toby screamed, as Guy began to lose blood at an alarming rate.

'Please,' Guy implored, 'please, God make me catch Toby's good blood!'

The younger brother drew his hand away and ran from the kitchen.

'Mummy! Mummy!' he wailed. 'Guy's cut! He's bleeding all over the floor! Mummy, give him his stuff! Quick!'

For a few moments, Guy stood alone in his own blood, while his hand spurted dangerously. He knew that he was not cured. His plan had not worked.

The next three days were spent in hospital.

*　*　*

Guy could delay the day no longer. The scar of the knifepoint, in the palm of his right hand, was the first thing he looked at. It was as permanent as his pain.

Today, though, he would have to rethink his plans, and full consciousness would be needed for that.

It was early spring, and Guy decided that a steady walk in the grounds after breakfast might help to clarify his thoughts.

The sun was summoning its first warmth of the year, and the buds on the trees were ready to burst forth, unleashing the colours which winter lacks. Guy was not aware of the day's beauty, however, such things were no longer a part of his world.

The wedding, being planned for early April, was almost upon him. Now, he must deal with Tessa before Janice Perry, and that would present problems.

'Guy!'

It was his next victim, running through the woods after him.

'Tessa? I didn't expect to see you this morning.'

'Your mother told me you were out here taking a walk. She and your father are making a short-list for the job of chauffeur — for you, I believe.'

'Oh that — mm — ridiculous, isn't it?'

'No, don't knock it, Guy. I wouldn't mind a chauffeur; you can lend him to me if you like.'

Guy laughed. He wished that he did not like Tessa Gregg.

'I've got a free day, and I wondered if you'd talk to me about your ill . . . I mean condition. We're doing blood next week. If you don't want to, I'll understand. It's entirely up to you, Guy.'

'Let's walk up to the well while we talk. Did you know we have a natural well? Has Toby shown you?'

'No, he hasn't.'

'Come on then, and I'll answer all your questions.'

'Right.' Tessa took Guy's arm. 'As long

178

as I'm not offending my future brother-in-law.'

Guy saw the possibility of a quick and easy killing. One push and that would be the end of Tessa Gregg and of any imperfect children she may have given life to.

'So, what do you want to know about haemophilia?'

'Well . . . as well as the obvious physical problems, we have to concentrate on possible emotional effects as well.'

'Good, I'm glad of that.'

Guy listened to Tessa's lilting voice. He found her enthusiasm for life disarming.

'That's why it's so useful to be able to talk to you, Guy. Clinical details can be read in any textbook, but nurses, in this day and age, have to be concerned with all aspects of the patient's well-being.'

'Very commendable.'

'So, do you feel that suffering from haemophilia has caused you to have any emotional problems? Not now — you're obviously very well-adjusted, but in the past, when you were a child perhaps?'

Guy pursed his lips.

179

'I suppose I had the occasional tantrum, when I was fed up with the endless injections, but that was all. I think I've always been a pretty stable sort of person . . . easy-going really.'

'It must make you quite tough, coping with a condition like that from a very early age.' Tessa spoke as though she was reading from a script.

'Yes, it does. I always consider myself to be a strong person — mentally and emotionally strong.'

Guy's mind was drifting.

'Nevertheless, things can't always have been easy for you, especially as Toby didn't have the condition. Weren't you ever jealous of him?'

'No — no — I don't think so. We've always been the best of friends — Toby and me.'

'Yes, he's very fond of you.' Tessa paused, then: 'Do you think you'll ever marry, Guy? Or will your condition cause you to remain a bachelor? Are you worried about passing the gene on — through any children you might have?'

'What?' Suddenly Guy's thoughts were rampaging — out of control. Tessa's voice was no more than a distant annoyance. They were approaching the track, which led to the well.

The prospect of killing in this near spontaneous manner was worrying to him. He had not had time to plan — to consider all aspects of Tessa's death. Guy was uneasy. This did not feel right.

'My goodness, that must be a fantastic daydream, you're having.' Tessa's words pierced Guy's consciousness. 'Or are you just sick of my questions?'

'Er . . . no, of course I'm not. Sorry — what did you say, Tess?'

'Will you ever marry and have children?'

'I won't marry, no. I decided that a long time ago. I shouldn't think that many women would want to spend their life with someone who'll need a great deal of looking after in later years. I'm becoming very dependent on my wheelchair already. As you can see, even on this short walk, I'm only able to saunter along. And yes, I would worry about passing a defective gene on to a future generation. So I shall never have children of my own.'

'Does that bother you?'

'No.'

'Not at all?'

'Not at all. I'm afraid you and Toby will have to continue the Dunbar line.'

'No, Guy. We won't be presenting you with any nieces or nephews.'

An extremely baffled Guy said nothing. He questioned Tessa, though, with his eyes, which searched her soul. She responded slowly.

'We — we said we wouldn't tell anyone. Toby would be furious if he knew I was talking like this, but I do feel so very close to you, Guy, even though we haven't known each other for very long.'

'So, you and Toby have decided never to have children. Well, that's your business. You'll probably change your mind in a few years, though, when you're bored with nursing the sick and moaning.' Guy awaited Tessa's reply, hoping for elucidation.

'No, it isn't that. I had an illness a

while back, and it's left me infertile. I suppose that's why I'm so desperate to make a success of my career. You won't tell anyone else, will you?'

'Of course I won't.'

Guy's mind was in chaos, though absolute tranquillity was all that Tessa saw.

'I'm so lucky to have found Toby,' she sighed. 'He doesn't mind at all — about not having children. He says that as long as he's got me it doesn't matter. I think your father will be pretty peeved, mind you.'

'Mm.' Guy was still absorbing the full implications of the situation.

'Toby says that your father must never be told. He says that, in years to come, he'll realize that we're going to be childless, and it'll be easier to accept. If we tell him now, though, we'll have to scrape him off the ceiling. I suggested that we should adopt, but Toby doesn't seem keen, and he says that Phillip wouldn't be in favour of adoption either.'

'No, he wouldn't.'

'Toby says he thinks of people as

though they were horses — you know — the development of the thoroughbred — the pedigree — the bloodline. A child that wasn't of his blood wouldn't be his grandchild, and he wouldn't want it to carry on his name.'

'Yes, Toby's right there, poor Dad. He must have been so relieved that his second son was normal — not defective, like me.'

'Oh no, Guy. Don't say things like that about yourself — please.'

'Why not? It's true. But now, even Toby won't be giving him the grandchild he wants — someone to inherit everything he's built up.'

'No, I'm afraid he won't.'

'Serves him right.'

'Sorry?'

'Dad — it serves him right for thinking like he does. He's a bit of a fascist, you know.'

'You will keep our secret, won't you, Guy?'

'Absolutely. It's no one else's business but yours anyway.'

'Thanks.'

Tessa kissed Guy's cheek. He was relieved that she was barren; it meant that he could allow her to live, and save Toby from his sorrow.

★ ★ ★

'Here's the well, Tessa — take a look down there.'

Tessa gripped the low stone wall and craned her neck to see what she could of the well's great depth.

'Ooh, I don't think I'll get too close,' she gasped, 'it's so deep! To be honest, it makes my stomach turn over. All that darkness — it's as if it goes on forever — nothing but darkness. It's scary.'

'Here, drop this stone and wait for the splash,' Guy urged, 'then you'll see how deep it is.'

Tessa held her breath as the stone plummeted down the well. It was several seconds before it broke the surface of the water.

'That's amazing!' she said, taking Guy's arm again. 'Come on, let's go back to the house.'

'Aren't you going to make a wish? Toby and I always used to when we came here.'

'No. I don't believe in wishes, Guy.'

'Neither do I.'

12

The first Saturday in April brought a chill breeze, but an optimistic brightness too.

Dunbar House was brimful with obscure relatives, whom Guy had not seen for years, and had no wish to encounter now. His mother and Aunt Kate were bustling around a nervous Toby. Guy, like his father, was trying to keep out of the way. Being the best man, however, he was coming in for an abundance of attention, especially with regard to his appearance.

The morning seemed longer than other mornings, and Guy was relieved when it was time for Toby and himself to leave for the village church. It was about a mile to old Darley Village, which lay in the opposite direction to Darley New Town, and, as the limousine coasted along the narrow lane, the two brothers savoured the quietness.

'You have got the rings, haven't you?'

Toby asked, as they arrived at the church.

'Safe as houses,' Guy replied, tapping the waistcoat pocket which held the small, golden tokens, and simultaneously replacing his top hat.

Tessa was not late for her wedding. As the other guests stared with admiration at the bride in her white gown and her flowing lace veil, Guy wanted to laugh. The utter stupidity of the ignorant masses never failed to amuse him, except, of course, when it angered him. There they stood, in hilarious hats and gruesome outfits, while Toby and Tessa took obsolete vows in the house of a dubious God. How absurd it all was.

The wedding reception was held in a large but select hotel near old Darley Village. Guy's speech was brief, and contained only a smattering of the expected humour. He left the longer and more pompous address to his father, who clearly enjoyed giving forth to such an amiable audience.

After the meal, speeches and endless toasts were completed. It was then time for the radiant new Mrs. Dunbar and her husband to lead their guests into the ballroom, where tables and chairs surrounded the highly polished dance floor. The bride and groom led the dancing, and, after a round of applause, were joined by Alex, Phillip and a few of their guests.

Guy sat with his Aunt Kate.

'Well,' Alex declared, half way through the celebrations, and with her voice raised slightly so that she would be heard above the music, 'it's all gone off very well, hasn't it?'

'Don't speak too soon,' Phillip warned, 'or they'll be running out of drinks, or something equally ridiculous.'

'They'd better not!' Alex insisted. 'Not with the amount of money this is costing!'

'It's all been splendid,' Aunt Kate assured. 'Now, how about a foxtrot, Guy? I'm too old to sit still all evening; my knees are stiffening up.'

'I'm not much of a one for dancing, Aunt Kate,' Guy replied, 'you know that.'

'Well, I'll let you off the foxtrot then, but I insist on the next waltz.'

Aunt Kate did not have to wait for long. Just a few minutes later, she and Guy were gliding around the dance floor with elegance on her part, but ineptitude on his.

Just as Guy was feeling relieved that the dance was coming to its end, an Uncle of Tessa's who had consumed rather too much of almost everything that was available, staggered across the floor and straight into him. The slippery surface caused Guy's feet to slide in all directions. Aunt Kate tried to help him, but it was no good, he fell heavily on to his left hip.

'Guy!' Alex screamed.

The ballroom fell silent. Nobody danced. Everybody stared.

Guy lay, awkward and so very humiliated, in the middle of the room.

'I'm all right,' he uttered to Aunt Kate, who attempted to help him to his feet.

'No!' Alex shouted, as she reached his side. 'Get an ambulance — quick! There might be some damage. Don't try to get him up. He must go to hospital.'

'I don't think I can stand up,' Guy

admitted, after trying to do so, but collapsing again.

'I knew you shouldn't be dancing,' Alex cried, 'I didn't want to fuss — not today of all days — but I knew you shouldn't be on this slippery floor.'

'I'll be all right, Mother,' Guy whispered, 'just stop everybody staring at me as if I'm some sort of freak in a circus. Get the band to start up again, Dad, for Christ's sake.'

Phillip and Toby gently carried Guy to the edge of the dance floor, while Aunt Kate instructed the band to resume playing. It was not until Guy had been taken out on a stretcher, however, that the party recommenced with any impetus.

Alex sat in the ambulance, clutching Guy's hand.

'They shouldn't have carried you like that,' she said, her lips tightening across her teeth, always a sign that she was annoyed. 'Your father and Toby should have known better.'

'They could see my embarrassment, Mother,' Guy answered tersely.

'Nevertheless, they should have waited

for the ambulance men.'

'Oh let it drop, Mother. We know it's just internal bleeding; I'll be fine once they've pumped some stuff into me.'

Alex changed the subject.

'Poor Tess,' she muttered, 'she's so upset about her uncle knocking you over.'

'Drunken slob!' Guy proclaimed.

'Yes, isn't he just. I feel sorry for Tess, though, on her special day too. Still, you'll be better soon, that's the main thing. Where does it hurt, darling? Just the hip?'

'Mm. That's where the pain's worst.'

'Poor love.'

Alex stroked Guy's hair from his moist forehead.

'Don't fuss, Mother, please. You should have stayed at the reception with Dad. There was no need for you to leave.'

'I couldn't possibly have stayed at the do while they took you off to hospital, Guy. As long as your father's there to see that everything goes smoothly, there's no need for me to stay too.'

Guy was in too much pain to argue.

That night, after tests and injections, it was explained to Guy and his mother, though they had both guessed anyway, that his hip was not broken, but badly bruised. For Guy, this meant heavy internal bleeding and several days in hospital.

At least, he deliberated, in an attempt to console himself he would not have to face the aftermath of the wedding. He would have time to think — time on his own.

* * *

By lunchtime the following day, Guy's private room was full of get-well cards, fruit and flowers. His pain was considerable, but he was accustomed to that. The treatment was familiar too. He had often paid such visits to hospital wards after minor injuries in his younger years. He could cope with all that. What was not so easy to deal with, was the memory of all those people at the wedding reception. If anyone else had slipped, it would have been a hand up, a laugh and incident forgotten, but it was so different because it was him. The instant he had fallen, all those who knew of his condition had immediately whispered the dreadful facts to those who were in ignorance. Guy could still see them — eyes and mouths wide — held in quiet horror by the spectacle of him sprawled on the dance floor, while his mother grew almost hysterical at his side. He had felt as though he was in a shop window. That herd of cretinous wretches would stay forged in his mind long after his injuries were healed. He would always see those thoughts behind their eyes: the concern, the kindness, but most of all, the pity. Guy wished that he could kill them all, so that they would not be able to remember his fragility and his weakness. He must rid their minds of those memories, so that when they thought of Guy Dunbar, they thought only of his strength and what he had taught them.

Once he was out of this place, they would know. They would soon be told of his mission.

Alex's visits were very frequent. Now that Toby and Tessa had gone away, Guy had her full attention again. Each time she came into his room, sometimes with his father, sometimes with Aunt Kate and sometimes alone, he could not deny that satisfaction — even delight — lifted his mind. And after each visit he reflected, in some detail, on the reason for this mild elation. He came to the conclusion that the joy he felt on seeing Alex was due partly to the fact that he adored her, but mainly to the fact that he could hate loving her all over again. Yes, that was it, he loathed the actual instinctive love that he could not avoid feeling for his mother, but this loathing, in itself, was eminently agreeable.

After two or three days, the time began to hang heavy, and Guy became impatient to get out of this disinfected hell, where suffering and death were the norm.

His parents brought in the proofs of the wedding photographs for his perusal, but his interest in them was negligible. He needed to do his work.

On the fifth morning of his enforced stay. Guy was wheeled to the X-ray department. At least it would make a change from the four pale blue walls of his room, with the nondescript water colours of some bleak seascape.

Guy was dumped in a fairly large waiting room with several doors leading off from it: X-ray, physiotherapy, haematology and so on. Ever since he was a child, Guy had avoided reading hospital notices, as far as possible; he found them strangely macabre.

He was not alone in the waiting room for long. Soon, another wheelchair entered. Guy was momentarily astounded. Its occupant was Janice Perry.

'Flaming awful places these, aren't they?' Janice struck up conversation with her future killer, directly the nurse had left the room.

'Yes — yes, they are,' Guy agreed, calming himself very competently and smiling warmly.

'I'm supposed to be going home tomorrow, about bloody time too. I'm sick of it in here.'

'You're going home?'

'Yes. I could've gone today, but I've got to wait and see some bloody specialist. I'm perfectly all right now, why they keep sitting me in this flaming wheelchair, I don't know. I've told them that I can walk on my own. They don't listen to you, do they?'

'No, not always, no.'

Janice's fingers danced erratically on her lap.

'Can't wait to get back to normal,' she went on, 'I really can't — back to work — see a bit of life.'

'Where do you work?'

'Dandy's nightclub. Good there it is — good disco — great atmosphere.'

'Really? I'll have to drop in some time.'

'I'm going straight back to work too — don't care what this lot say. They don't know everything, do they? I'd be climbing up the walls if I sat indoors every night. I'd be bored out of my tree. Christ, I wish I could have a fag!'

'Back to normal,' Guy muttered forlornly.

'Eh? Yes — back to normal tomorrow, I can't wait. What about you? You in for long? Sounds like you're inside, doesn't it? Might as well be in clink — not much different in these places, is it? When are you going home?'

'Soon. Should be within the next few days.'

'That's good.'

'Yes, I'm going home — but back to normal — that's a different matter altogether.'

'Eh?'

The nervy Janice twitched when she did not fully understand. Guy enjoyed her bewilderment — her stupidity. It made him want to attack her.

'Some of us never live lives that are normal,' he explained arrogantly.

'Oh, I see. You're stuck in that bloody thing, are you?' Janice pointed to Guy's wheelchair.

'I'm afraid there's much more to it than that,' he replied, 'the wheelchair will be the final insult — the final curse. Life is all darkness for people like me . . . one long, dark struggle.'

The young woman began to bite her fingernails.

'Here comes that bloody nurse,' she whispered to Guy. 'She's so flippin' cheerful, I'd like to throttle her, I really would.'

Guy smiled.

The nurse came out of the physio-therapy room.

'Come on, Janice,' she chirped, 'your turn for the skylark!'

Janice looked at Guy as she was wheeled past him, and her eyes retreated to the top of their sockets with contemptuous weariness.

Guy smothered a giggle.

So, Janice Perry would be back at work in a day or two. That information was just the tonic he needed.

Once back in his bed, Guy wondered whether he should take the opportunity offered by fate, and murder her in her sleep that night. Pillow over the face — asphyxiation — what could be easier? Janice Perry, however, would not be in a private ward. Too many eyes, he decided, too many potential witnesses. Anyway, it would be too easy for her. She must know — she must suffer. Yes, he would execute her when she was alone; when he could talk to her. The time would soon come now. He could wait a little longer — he would have his second victory.

When his mother visited him later that day, Guy was scarcely aware of her presence. He wanted only to be alone — to anticipate the coming joy.

Guy slept soundly that night. Contentment was his.

13

In the event, it was almost a week after his discharge from hospital before Guy's hip had healed enough for him to undertake the night ride to Darley New Town. He cycled slowly, and went straight to Janice Perry's street. The flat above the grocer's was in darkness, so he surmised that she must have gone to work at Dandy's. He hid Toby's bicycle in a nearby street, and himself in the deep porch, which protected Janice's front door. There would be no chase through the streets this time — no physical pain. He would simply sit and wait for her.

He had taken the knife and the towel from their hiding place in his cupboard, donned the plastic mack which he had bought several weeks before and put on an old pair of leather gloves. A thick, waterproof carrier bag, which had carried his murderer's garb and the weapon, was now folded in the pocket of his shapeless mackintosh.

Guy sat at the very back of the porch, leaning against Janice's front door. It was pitch-black there, the porch being a good eight feet deep, not that anybody was around anyway, in that miserable side street in the early hours of the morning.

It was not too cold, this night in mid April, and Guy found it very pleasant, sitting there, relaxed and waiting to kill.

At about twenty minutes to three, he heard a distant clinking. Those spindly stiletto heels announced the coming of his second victim. He stood up. This time the knife was in his right hand, just to confuse the police a little. He was calm and strong. The clinking grew louder; she was almost there.

The heels stopped. Her frame appeared in the doorway. She fumbled in her bag for her key, and then stepped into the absolute darkness of the porch, a darkness so onerous that you could almost touch it.

Guy grabbed her and pushed her against the door. His hand firmly covered her mouth and the weight of his body held her puny limbs still. Janice tried to manoeuvre her floundering right hand up to the yale lock, but the key fell from her indecisive fingers. This loss seemed to trigger something in the young woman. Suddenly she fought and struggled like a demented savage, but with Guy's weight against her back, there was little she could achieve. He pushed the knife just a little way into the side of her scrawny neck, and could just see her healthy blood trickling exactly as Joanna's had done.

'What about your little son?' Guy whispered, turning his prey to face him and then pushing the knife a little deeper. 'What about Andrew?'

Janice fought a moment longer, but the intense dread and panic which had gripped her caused her to vomit, and with Guy's hand covering her mouth, she began to choke. Guy withdrew the knife from her neck and quickly pushed it hard into her chest. He wanted his action — his knife — to be the direct cause of her death — not a windpipe full of vomited booze. As Janice collapsed, her breathing obstructed and the newly made opening in her chest billowing forth her life-blood, she did not have time to wonder why. She slid to her death knowing nothing but terror.

Guy was euphoric. He had succeeded. Looking at the repugnant state of the late Janice Perry, amid her warm blood and recently emitted vomit, he decided that she had been stripped of all dignity — all humanity — and he alone was responsible. How very fitting that was.

Guy took the plastic bag from his pocket and put the knife in it. He tiptoed through the quickly cooling blood, and then, when he could step onto the dry pavement, he took off his shoes and put them in the bag too. He removed his mack, and the bloody garment also landed in the sturdy, plastic receptacle, as did the towel, when he had wrapped his gloves in it.

After taking one more satisfied glance back at Janice Perry's body, Guy walked in his stocking feet to Toby's cycle. The saddlebag, being quickly filled with the evidence of his night's enjoyment, Guy rode slowly back to Dunbar House.

His feet felt a little sore on the pedals, but nothing to give him concern. His present mood could not be marred by the fact that he was shoeless.

* * *

He rode Toby's bike into the woods and up to the well. Then, the debris from the murder of Janice Perry joined that from the murder of Joanna Coles.

14

'The milkman found her,' Sergeant Skinner explained to Chief Inspector Blaire, 'at about six o' clock. He's in a bit of a state, I'm afraid. One of the neighbours has taken him in — giving him a cup of tea, I think. The victim's name is Janice Perry, so the neighbour says.'

'Right, I'll speak to the milkman and the neighbour in a minute.'

The usually obscure little back street was enjoying its new found fame, as the insipid rays of the early sun lifted the curtain on police cordons, curious spectators and the numerous experts who crawl around the scenes of such hideous crimes.

Around the body, the iron smell of cold blood combined with the stench of stale vomit, the main constituent of which was alcohol.

'I'll obviously be able to tell you more

when we've done our business at the lab,' the pathologist explained, 'but first impressions are that she's been dead for four or five hours. Cause of death — this deeper knife wound in the chest, or possibly, obstruction of the windpipe — we'll let you know for certain when we've opened her up. No apparent sexual assault.'

'Any next of kin found?' Silas Blaire asked Sergeant Skinner.

'No, sir, not yet. We've contacted the owner of the shop — he's her landlord. He'll be here in a minute. Unfortunately, he couldn't help us as far as the relatives are concerned though. Her purse is still in her bag, by the way. The motive clearly wasn't robbery.'

'I see.' Chief Inspector Blaire, stooping over Janice's body, turned his face up to his sergeant. 'Well, bells should be clanging — never mind ringing!' he said. 'Anything strike you about this murder?'

'Yes, sir. No sexual motive, no robbery and the two knife wounds — it's obvious — Joanna Coles.'

'That's right, Sergeant Skinner.' Silas

Blaire straightened up. 'We have the smaller knife wound in the neck, and then the larger wound — the one meant to kill — deep in the chest. We also have no apparent motive. We can't be absolutely certain yet, not until the forensic boys have finished, but I think that Joanna Coles and Janice Perry were killed by the same man. And we've got to find him — and find him pretty damned quick.'

The milkman was of little use to the investigating officers. He had found Janice, there in the porch, when delivering her pint of full cream milk. She was sometimes a bit short of cash — late paying her bill — but that was all he knew about her.

Mr. Allsworth, the owner of the shop and Janice's landlord, was able to tell Silas Blaire that the deceased woman worked at Dandy's nightclub, and that she had been his tenant for six or seven years. He knew nothing about her relatives, however. She had never talked to him about parents, brothers or sisters or anyone else. She had always seemed to be alone in the world.

'You know, Skinner,' Silas Blaire confessed, as the young woman's body was zipped into the body bag for its journey to the mortuary, 'one of the most hateful parts of our job is informing relatives about the death of a loved-one. But, when there's no one to tell — no one to mourn — it cuts me in half, and I don't mind admitting it. There doesn't seem to be anybody to miss this young woman, and that's so sad, don't you think?'

'Yes, sir, very sad.'

'Still, back to business. The more I look at this crime, the more I think it's his second murder — Joanna Coles being his first. You see how he's cleared up after himself. In all this mess, there's no trace of him. He must have cleaned his shoes thoroughly or removed them altogether, to avoid leaving bloody footprints on this pavement. It's all been planned again, Skinner. He brought the murder weapon with him and possibly protective clothing too. I'll bet the boys don't find any fingerprints on her or in that porch, and I'll lay money there's nothing under her nails — no fibres, skin or hair. He probably pinned her arms by her sides with his body weight and wore plastic — or some other material with no fibres. I should say he wore leather or rubber gloves too. It's got to be Joanna Coles's murderer. Neither woman was heard to scream, so he must have covered their mouths somehow, but their was no sign of anything on Joanna Coles's face or inside her mouth to suggest that tape of any kind had been used. It'll be the same with this woman too; I'm sure of it. He covers the mouth with a gloved hand — a glove with no fibres.'

'But why these two women? If he plans it all so carefully, would he murder at random? Or does he choose his victims for a specific reason?'

'Oh I think there's a reason, Skinner, but what the devil it is ... ask me another!'

★   ★   ★

'Bit of a problem, sir,' Sergeant Skinner announced, as he entered the incident

210

room later that day, clutching the pathologist's report.

'Oh?'

'Yes. You remember that Joanna Coles's murderer was left-handed?'

'Yes, I remember that, Skinner. Why, had you forgotten?'

'Well, no sir. But the thing is, Janice Perry's killer was right-handed.'

Silas Blaire said nothing until he had read the pathologist's findings.

'He's playing with us, Skinner,' the Chief Inspector concluded. 'Have you read this?'

'Not all of it, I brought it straight to you.'

'Well, everything points to the same man having murdered both women — except for the hand used.'

'And you don't think that's important, sir?'

'I don't think we have one left-handed killer and one right-handed killer. I believe we have one man who used his left hand when murdering Joanna Coles and his right hand when murdering Janice Perry. He's trying to confuse the issue,

Skinner, but it's the same man all right. And he needn't think we're that bloody stupid!'

'So, this second murder changes everything.'

'Absolutely. We're no longer looking for a man with an obsession for, or grudge against, Joanna Coles, but for someone with a reason for murdering both these women.'

'So, Peter Barnett and Michael Gilchrist are off the hook?'

'They were never really on it, Skinner. We will, of course, check that neither of them had any connection with Janice Perry, but I'm pretty certain we'll find that they didn't know her from Eve.'

'So where do we start, sir?'

'We'll get Geoff Dixon to give us a hand. It's surprising what these psychologists can come up with in such cases. He's a damned good bloke too. And, naturally, Skinner, we'll talk to anyone and everyone who might possibly know something that could be useful. This man must be stopped before he kills again.'

★　★　★

It was the following morning, a Saturday, when Silas Blaire and John Skinner arrived on the doorstep of Jean and Peter Barnett. The two policemen were greeted by Jean, who showed them into the lounge. From the freshness of the scent which lingered in her wake, Silas supposed that she had recently bathed. He was physically attracted to Jean Barnett, and this admission, albeit only to himself, unnerved him.

'We wondered if we could have a word with your husband, Mrs. Barnett,' Silas explained.

'You don't think he was involved with this girl who was murdered, do you?' she blustered, her angry mood causing her face to blush like a young girl's. 'I know he was stupid sending that letter to Joanna, but he didn't kill her — and he certainly didn't murder this other one — he's been up in Edinburgh for almost a week!'

'Edinburgh?'

'Yes, Chief Inspector Blaire — Edinburgh. You see, since Peter told me about his infatuation for Joanna, and that wretched letter, things haven't been too good between us. Call me silly, if you like, but I can't accept that my husband was that attracted to another woman. And, unfortunately, I'm not the sort of person who takes such insults — because I do consider it to be a personal insult to me — without a bit of fuss. Anyway, the upshot of all the rows is that we decided a few days apart might help matters. So, Peter has been staying with his only sister, and her family, in Edinburgh . . . all right?'

'Yes, thank you, Mrs. Barnett.'

'Is that a good enough alibi, Chief Inspector Blaire?'

'We really only wanted to eliminate your husband from our inquiries, Mrs. Barnett . . . just doing our job . . . we do have two murdered women, you understand.'

Silas Blaire's assertive attitude quickly placated Jean; her agitation subsided. She realized that he deemed her grievances to be somewhat petty, when considered alongside the two vicious murders he was investigating.

'Yes, I know, Chief Inspector,' she replied, feeling puerile, and wishing that she had shown this man a different, if less typical side of her personality. 'I do understand that you have a difficult job to do.'

'Well that's Barnett in the clear,' John Skinner said, as he drove his superior officer to the other side of town.

'Yes, as far as we're concerned anyway.'

'Mm . . . sorry?'

'I don't think that Mrs. Barnett will be so ready to accept his word about anything anymore . . . no, Peter Barnett will be in the dock for some time to come.'

Sergeant Skinner grinned.

'I think I'll stay single,' he muttered.

* * *

'He's not there!' Michael Gilchrist's next door neighbour called, as the Chief Inspector and his sergeant walked up the lone father's garden path. 'He told me he was going away for a couple of days — something to do with Giles's school. He went on Thursday.'

215

'Right, thanks very much!' Sergeant Skinner called.

'I don't know why you can't leave the poor bastard alone,' came the neighbour's surly retort, 'he's only trying to do the best for his boy — trying to get on with his life.'

Feeling suitably chastised, the two policemen returned to their car and made straight for Darley Hill Special School.

The headmistress, who was helping to organize a jumble sale in the school hall, explained that Michael Gilchrist had gone with a few other parents, two teachers and several handicapped pupils to a special outward bound centre in Wales. Apparently, this was an annual event, and it was the third time that Michael Gilchrist and Giles had gone on the trip.

'I'm glad he's in the clear,' Silas Blaire said, his relief being hardly discernable. 'I didn't think he had anything to do with either murder, but it's good to know for certain. Right, now let's see what Geoff Dixon has come up with. He should be at the station going through all the reports as we speak.'

*   *   *

Geoff Dixon, the psychologist who gave specialist help to the Darley New Town police when it was required, was short, fat and bald. He had an impenetrable auburn beard, which made the absence of hair on his head far more noticeable than it would otherwise have been. His brown eyes were embedded in loose, wrinkled skin, and he appeared older than his forty-two years.

'Can't manage without me then, Silas?' he joked, as the two friends shook hands.

Next, Sergeant Skinner was introduced to the genial little man.

'So, what can you tell us about this chap?' Silas Blaire asked. 'I don't mind admitting that we haven't got a great deal to go on so far.'

'Well, he's extremely organized and methodical about his crimes, but I'm sure you've gathered that much yourselves. He's confident too — that business with the knife — using different hands to kill each woman — I'd say he's enjoying what he's doing and teasing the police is a part of his pleasure.'

'Will he kill again?' Silas Blaire asked the vital question.

'Oh yes. He's trying to tell us something. He won't stop until he gets his message over.'

'How do you know that?' Sergeant Skinner put in.

'Because there appears to be no motive — no sexual assault and no robbery — yet he's chosen these two women and he's chosen them for a reason. We know he didn't just murder at random, because he went to Joanna Coles's house on the one evening in the week when her husband was not there. He knew that she would be alone, and he was confident that he could gain entry to her house. As for Janice Perry, nobody would hang around in that little back street, in the early hours, on the off chance that a woman would walk past. There are far more likely areas that he could have chosen. No, he either knew her, or he'd watched her. He waited in the street, probably hidden at the back of that porch, at about the time he knew she would be coming home from her place of work. He knew the routines of both these women, and he planned their murder because they were who they were. There's nothing spontaneous or random about either of these crimes. I think he wants to let us all know how he feels about something — possibly something that, to us, is of no importance at all, but to his obsessive mind is the only thing in his life that matters.'

'Why these two women, though?' Silas pondered aloud. 'Joanna Coles let him into her house — we're fairly certain that she knew him.'

'Yes, very possibly she did, just as Janice Perry might have known him. I'm pretty certain, though, that there's something about his victims which links them in their murderer's mind. Possibly there's something about them which he so abhors that he is driven to eliminate them, so teaching the rest of mankind that we'd be better off without such women.'

'What turns people into psychopaths?' Sergeant Skinner asked. 'I mean, how does it really happen?'

'There isn't one rule, John,' the psychologist replied, as though he'd known the young policeman all his life. 'It would make the identification of these people a lot easier if there were. We know that certain personality types are more prone to such behaviour than others, and we know that the environment and the experiences which a child encounters in its formative years can foster sociopathic tendencies, but there is still a lot to learn — still a great deal we don't know. Some people may simply be born psychopaths.'

'Well, I can think of a hell of a lot of differences between the two women,' Silas Blaire declared, flicking through the pertinent files, 'but nothing that I'd call a link between them.'

'Mm,' agreed Geoff Dixon thoughtfully. 'One in her thirties, one in her twenties. One married with a family, one who appears to have no family at all. They do completely different jobs, and seem to have diverse backgrounds.'

'Could he have seen something in their appearance?' John Skinner suggested tentatively. 'You know, something that reminded him of the mother that deserted him when he was six years old

— something like that.'

'They weren't that similar,' Geoff Dixon answered, 'not similar enough for a physical attribute to be the reason he singled them out anyway. Joanna Coles was clearly quite a beauty, but poor Janice didn't have a great deal going for her in the looks department, did she? Joanna had dark hair and Janice's was light brown with bleached streaks. They had different eye-colour too. They were both slim and not very tall, which would have made the attack itself somewhat easier — the average man could have held them down without too much difficulty. But no, I don't think there's anything in their appearance which would have linked them in the killer's eyes.'

'Not easy, this one,' Silas Blaire murmured, as much to himself as to his colleagues. 'We got virtually nothing from the scene of the crime in either case.'

'I see he used a different knife,' the psychologist remarked, 'probably disposed of the first one after he'd used it on Joanna Coles. Common blade types, though, no joy there. The wounds are quite interesting, however, both women having the smaller wound on the side of the neck, and the deep wound — the fatal one — in the chest.'

'Yes, what do you make of that, Geoff?' Silas asked. 'I thought that perhaps the small wound in the neck was to keep the victim still — you're less likely to struggle if you feel a knife piercing your skin, I should imagine.'

'Possibly, but let's take that a step further, Silas. Why didn't he simply stab them in the chest and be done with it? Why did he need to keep them still before he actually got round to killing them?'

'You tell me.'

'I think he wanted to talk to them. He put the knife in the neck to paralyze them with fear, and he told them exactly why he was about to murder them. There's no doubt that he enjoyed their terror, and the small wound allowed him to punish them for that little bit longer, though what for . . . God only knows.'

'So,' John Skinner said, with sedate resolve, 'we search for a link between the victims, and hope it leads us to the killer before the sadistic bastard decides to kill again.'

'That's about it,' Geoff Dixon replied, 'and I should imagine, now that he's murdered twice, that his confidence is growing. He may not take so long between killings next time.'

★ ★ ★

That evening, Silas Blaire and John Skinner entered Dandy's at about nine o'clock.

Tracey Delahay, one of the barmaids, was eager to talk to the policemen.

'It was a few weeks ago now,' she explained, 'I walked home with Janice one night, and the next day, she told me that, after I'd left her, she spotted a bloke following her.'

'Did she say that she knew him?' Silas Blaire asked hopefully.

'No — it was so dark that she couldn't see his face — he was quite a way behind her apparently. I believe she said that he had a bicycle.'

'Did you always walk home with Janice

Perry, Miss Delahay?'

'No. I don't do as many nights as she does — did.'

'Was she nervous after that night?'

'Yes. She said he almost caught her up, but luckily she got through her front door before he reached her.'

'And he was on a bike?' Silas Blaire was clearly confused.

'No — no, Janice said he was pushing the bike — I'm sure she did.'

'Not riding it?'

'No.'

'I see.'

'I don't. I remember thinking, when she told me, that he must have been a nutter not to get on the bike. He'd have caught her if he had — no trouble.'

'Did she continue to walk home alone after this business?'

'Not at first, no. She started getting a taxi every night — we shared when I was here too. Then she had that spell in hospital. I suppose she decided she'd walk again once she came back to work. Taxis do get expensive, and I told her that I'd never seen anybody about — not while she was in hospital, that is.'

'Did Janice ever talk of her family, Miss Delahay, or anyone at all that she was close to?'

'No. I always felt sorry for her really. She was a bit of a loner. Her mother went off and left her with her dad, I believe, when she was very young. He beat her about till the authorities put her in care. That's what I gathered anyway; she hardly ever talked about it. I don't think she had any family left at all — she always seemed to be on her own. And now this . . . not much of a life, was it?'

*   *   *

'Do you think that was the killer, sir?' Sergeant Skinner asked, as they left the club, having spoken to each member of staff and finding out nothing more of any importance about Janice Perry.

'Our friend on the bike?'

'Mm.'

'It could have been, but with absolutely no description, it isn't much help, is it? We could do a door-to-door in the area, but, as it happened weeks ago, and in the middle of the night too, I shouldn't think we'd get a lot of joy — still, it's all we've got at present — organize it, will you, Skinner — just in case we get lucky. And put something out on the news too, especially the local news. Has anybody else been followed or approached in the area over the past few weeks — you know the sort of thing. If he was after Janice Perry, and nobody else, though, I can't see any help from that quarter either — still, it's . . . '

'Yes, sir, I know — it's all we've got.'

'And while you organize all that, Skinner, I shall go through the files yet again.'

15

A few days after his return from the trip to Wales with Darley Hill Special School, Michael Gilchrist accosted Dorothy Ballard in his son's classroom.

'I wanted to tell you personally,' he explained, as though feeling premature remorse about his intended actions. 'We're moving away from here — Giles and me.'

'Oh no, Michael — why?'

'Because of Joanna's murder — I mean that's when all the trouble started, isn't it? That's the reason for it.'

'But you're not a suspect, Michael. You never were — not really.'

'Well that isn't the way it felt, Dorothy.'

'Anyway, now that the other girl's been murdered, while you were away with the school, they can't possibly think . . . '

'Yes, I know. They believe me now — now that the damage has been done — now that everyone in the district is suspicious about me.'

'You're just imagining that, Michael, I'm sure of it. Nobody who knows you could possibly think that you'd hurt anybody.'

'Mud sticks, Dorothy. People I've known for years pass me in the street and pretend they haven't seen me. It only takes a few neighbours to see the police visiting, you know. Soon the odd whispered speculation gets passed around and exaggerated. Before you know it, the rumours are teeming around the district, and they aren't just going to evaporate either.'

'In a few week's time, nobody will even link you with the crime — not for a second. People do forget, and it won't take them long.'

'No, it's no good. I just can't cope. I've got to go to a new area and make a fresh start. All the time I'm here, I'll feel as though everyone is talking about me and pointing at me. Strangely enough, it doesn't matter very much whether they're saying that I'm the man who murdered Joanna Coles or that I'm the man who was cleared of her murder. It should matter, but it doesn't. I'll always be connected, in the minds of people round here, with that gruesome, bloody killing, and the only thing I can do is take Giles and myself right away from Darley New Town.'

'Well, if you've decided . . . I'm so sorry, though, . . . we'll miss you, and Giles too, of course.'

'I'm selling the house, and then I'll have to set about organizing a new school for Giles, hopefully in the country somewhere. I'd like to move to Derby-shire, or Yorkshire perhaps. It would be good for Giles to grow up in truly rural surroundings. Anyway, Dorothy, I'll let you and the headmistress know directly I have any definite news.'

'Yes, Michael, and I hope that, wherever you go, it will all work out for the best — for both of you.'

As Dorothy Ballard watched the hounded and innocent Michael Gilchrist leave her classroom, she wished, with frighteningly earnest shame, that she had never told Silas Blaire of that silly flirtation at the Christmas party. She had caused Michael so much anxiety and, as long as she lived, she would always regret that. Now, all she could hope was that the great upheaval before him would do Giles no lasting harm. He was so settled and so happy at Darley Hill with all his friends around him.

Dorothy's eyes were suddenly moist. She should not take all the blame for these sad events, however, she reminded herself, the true creator of the lamentable circumstances which now prevailed, was the murderer of Joanna Coles.

Dorothy Ballard quietly set about preparing her lessons for the following day. She needed to occupy her thoughts with mundane and familiar things.

★ ★ ★

When Peter Barnett had telephoned Stuart Coles and arranged to meet him in the saloon bar of the Darley Arms, the latter had wondered why.

'I felt that I wanted to talk to you,' Peter confessed awkwardly. 'There's been something on my mind — bothering me — and I need to put things straight.'

'I'm listening,' Stuart urged, realizing now what was causing Peter's agitation.

'Did you find a letter, Stuart?'

'Letter?' Stuart Coles's innate kindness overcame that side of his personality, which wanted to punish Peter for his ridiculous advances to his dear, dead Joanna.

'I wrote a letter to Joanna,' Peter admitted, 'only the one — and I was very drunk at the time. I wouldn't have written it if I'd been sober.'

'I don't think she told me about any letter,' Stuart lied. 'Why, what was it about? Was it important?'

'I — I just asked if I could meet her. I wanted to talk to her alone.'

'What about?'

'I suppose I was flirting with her, Stuart.' Peter's tone was at once apologetic and forthright.

'I see.'

'I thought that the police might have shown you the letter, or that you'd found it in Joanna's things, and I didn't want you to get the wrong idea. I didn't want you to have any more misery piled on you than you've already got — especially not because of that bloody stupid letter. Honestly, Stuart, I swear to you, it was only the drink. I mean, I did think that Joanna was extremely attractive — she was — but nothing at all happened between us — absolutely nothing.'

'Well, that's all right then,' Stuart said, wishing to end this rather inadequate man's misery, as soon as possible.

'Is that all you're going to say about it?' Peter asked, clearly astounded by Stuart's reaction to his confession.

'Yes, that's all.' Peter smiled. 'Look,' he went on, 'I knew Joanna better than anyone else could ever have known her. I'll tell you what happened, shall I? She received your letter, and realized that you would be regretting the fact that you'd ever written it. She'd have known that it was done in a moment of stupidity. I should imagine she came to see you about it — when Jean wasn't around, of course. She probably told you, very gently, that she would forget all about the silly note, and pretend that you'd never written it. Joanna loved me, Peter, and she told you so, I should think, reminding you that you loved Jean too. After that, she would have kept her word and treated you as though no letter had ever been sent. Is that roughly what happened?'

'Yes, Stuart, that's exactly what happened.'

'Right, well, I'll follow Joanna's example and forget all about it too.'

Peter bowed his head.

'I'm glad I've got that off my conscience before I go,' he said.

'Go? Are you and Jean moving away then?'

'No — just me.'

'What?'

'Jean and I are getting a divorce. I've been up in Scotland for a week or two — my sister and her family live up there. I'm lucky really, my firm have given me a transfer to the Edinburgh office, and I'm going to stay with my sister until I get myself settled in a flat.'

'Oh, Peter, I'm so sorry.'

'Yes, well Jean couldn't forgive me for

writing that letter, I'm afraid. She says that I wanted to deceive her, and that she could never trust me again. No trust — no love is her philosophy. Perhaps she's right — I don't know any more. We can't go on as we have been recently, though. I know that much. I'm catching the train to Scotland first thing in the morning; that's why I wanted to see you today.'

'Would it help if I spoke to Jean, do you think? If I explain to her just how trivial it all was . . . I'm willing to try, if you think it would do any good.'

'Thanks, Stuart, but I'm sure it wouldn't make any difference. You couldn't say anything that I haven't said fifty times over.'

'No — but coming from somebody else, she might take more notice — you never know.'

'It wouldn't work — really.'

'Well, if you say so.'

Peter went to the bar for another two beers, and on his return, he changed the subject.

'Now, how are you getting on?' he

asked sympathetically. 'We've been talking far too much about me, Stuart. You're the one with more to feel hurt and angry about than the rest of us put together.'

'Oh, I'm coping — just. There have been times — soon after the murder in particular — when I felt like throwing myself under a bus — not now though, so I suppose things must be getting a little better. You go on for the children, really, at first anyway. I had to remind myself that, just as I'd lost my wife, they had lost their mother. I couldn't deprive them of their father too, so here we all are, struggling on.'

'It must be so awful for you.'

'Yes, we're like three lost souls really. Three lost souls with no refuge — no sanctuary from the pain.'

'How do you manage with Ben? And your job and everything?'

'The bank has been very good about it all. I've had pretty flexible hours so far, although things are getting back to normal now. My mother and father have been marvellous with Ben — well, with both the children. I don't know what I would have done without them. Dad does a lot of the school runs for me and Mum cooks and cleans. They deserve a medal, they really do.'

'That's what families are all about though, isn't it? I'm pretty glad I've got a sister at the moment.' Peter paused. 'When I think of the way life's treated you,' he continued, 'the way you lost Joanna and everything, it makes me feel that Jean and I need our backsides kicking for the way we're splitting up. We've destroyed our marriage ourselves, whereas yours was wrecked in the cruelest way, through no fault of your own. When we're together, though, Jean and I, there just doesn't seem to be a way out of our problems. Isn't that pathetic?'

'There are all kinds of tragedies, Peter.'

'Yes, but ours is largely self-inflicted.'

'Little Sammy is a real trooper,' Stuart said, returning to his own thoughts. 'She's a tough one too, thank goodness. It's surprising how much she helps with Ben now; he relies on her quite a lot. I don't know if that's a good thing or not — I mean, it's all right now, but as she gets older, she'll want her own life, and quite rightly too. It's the future that really worries me, as far as Ben is concerned. The trouble is that I've got no one to share my worries with now, not like I used to share things with Joanna anyway. Still, it's no good harping on these things, is it?'

'I hope they get him soon, Stuart, the man that murdered Joanna — I really hope they do. He's ruined an awful lot of lives, in one way and another, but no one's more than yours.'

'Yes, I'd like five minutes alone with the bastard, believe me. But, as my mother says, that kind of bitterness and longing for revenge will only destroy me — and I know she's right — she always is. Mothers are a very special breed, aren't they? Very special.'

16

While the police of Darley New Town investigated the two murders which had shocked the district, the murderer's life was becoming more difficult to endure with every day that passed.

Guy's anguish had nothing to do with the lives, which he had ended so prematurely and mercilessly, on the contrary, thoughts of these victories afforded him the only delight which seemed accessible to him at this time. No, his misery was derived from the fact that his physical condition was deteriorating rapidly. To have any mobility at all, even within Dunbar House, Guy was now compelled to use his wheelchair. He was becoming grudgingly thankful that he had a car and chauffeur at his disposal, though he never said as much.

Toby and Tessa, having returned sun-tanned and happy from their honeymoon, were busy settling into the cottage, which Phillip had bought for them. It was only two miles from Dunbar House. Guy still saw Toby sometimes because Phillip and his younger son continued to work closely together, but it was not the same as when Toby had lived at home. Guy missed his brother.

'The cottage is looking lovely, Guy,' Alex enthused, as mother and son took coffee in the kitchen of Dunbar House. 'Tess has very good taste — she's doing the interior herself, you know. Toby's got a good one there. You should get Richard to drive you down and you could have a look round. Tess would love to see you — or I'll take you if you want me to — you know that.'

'Mm.'

Guy could not have been less interested and he made no attempt to hide the fact.

'Aches and pains tiresome, are they, darling?'

'No more than usual.'

'Paul said he'd like you to pop into the surgery and see him. Of course he'll visit you, if you don't feel up to it, but with Richard to drive you . . . '

'Mother,' Guy halted Alex mid-sentence.
'Yes?'

'Has Paul got a cure for haemophilia?'

'Well no, darling, you know he hasn't.'

'Can he get me out of this wheelchair and living a normal life?'

'Oh, Guy — don't please.'

'Then I don't think I'll bother to visit the useless bugger!'

'Guy! Paul has been very good to you over the years. Don't talk like that, please. I know you're in pain, darling, but it isn't Paul's fault, is it?'

Alex left the room to answer the telephone, which was ringing persistently in the hall.

'No, it isn't Paul's fault,' Guy muttered to himself, a louring wildness present in his eyes and his words.

★ ★ ★

Quite suddenly, Guy was sitting at the large table in the breakfast room. There were decorations and lots of food. It was Toby's sixth, or perhaps seventh birthday party, and he had just blown out his candles. The noise which emanated from Toby's school-friends was quite alarming to Guy, who rarely mixed with other children in such large numbers.

'You're ill, aren't you?' asked Adrian, a small seven year old with big ears and a rat's face.

Guy remembered his indignation still.

'No! I'm not ill!'

'My mother said you're ill. She said that's why you don't come to school with Toby.'

'Well she's wrong — your mother is. I'm a haemophiliac, and haemophilia is a condition, not an illness.'

'Same thing.'

'No it isn't, Adrian! It isn't the same thing at all!'

'My mother says she doesn't know how your mother can cope. I heard her telling my auntie . . . because my mother says that your mother gave you your himflipia. My mother said that it must be awful to know that you've given your child a terrible illness like you've got.'

'That's silly, Adrian. My mother would never make me ill — she loves me.'

'She did make you ill. It's because of her that you've got that himflipia. My mother said so and my mother knows because she's a nurse.'

When you are eight or nine years old, and the strongest bond of love and devotion which has formed in your short, vulnerable life is, quite brutally, thrown into question, it is not easy to forget the pain. Once more that very pain lived in Guy's heart. His security and his stability were gone. He was wide open to all the adversity with which the world could assault him. There was no safety anywhere — no shield surrounding Guy — no motherly protection — not from his darling mother. The agony that was his life was all her fault.

★ ★ ★

Soon she would pay though. Now that he was able to have his revenge, it would be so much more than simply sweet. She would be paying an enormous debt — a debt that she had owed to him since the moment of his conception.

The fact that Alex had not been aware that she carried that evil gene, made no difference at all to Guy . . . it never had done. It was all because of her . . . that was all he knew . . . all he wanted to know.

Guy glided along the main hallway and into his rooms. He heaved himself from his wheelchair and then limped across his bedroom to lie on his bed.

He would not use a knife on his mother, he decided. There would be no need to explain to her the reasons for his actions; she knew exactly what she was guilty of.

After her execution, Guy deliberated, he would be free. He would tell the world his message, and everyone would learn from his deeds. Little Andrew Perry and Ben Coles had already been avenged — but his own mother — that would show that his cause was a truly unselfish one.

Guy had decided that Alex would die in three day's time, when his father was on a buying trip to Southern Ireland. There would be no gloves — no cleaning up

— no anonymity — not this time. At last he would be able to claim the credit for what he had done.

The method he would use for her murder would be simple. He would go to his mother's room in the early hours, and bring a heavy brass paperweight crashing down onto her temple. To make absolutely certain that she was dead, he would then hold a pillow over her unconscious face for some minutes. The thought of this triumphant moment to come caused a smile to light Guy's face. He would sleep now, in a cocoon of warm, rapturous anticipation.

17

On the morning of the day that Guy
Dunbar had chosen for his mother's
death, Silas Blaire and John Skinner stood
in Janice Perry's sparsely furnished flat.
Yet again, they had ferreted about in the
murdered woman's shabby belongings
and, yet again, they had found nothing of
any use to their investigation. On this
occasion, Geoff Dixon had accompanied
them to the flat.

'We're missing something,' Silas con-
firmed to his colleagues, who needed no
telling. 'There's a link of some sort
between Janice Perry and Joanna Coles,
and we can't see it.'

'We need a clearer picture of Janice
Perry's life,' Geoff Dixon said, sitting on
the edge of the bed. 'There's not enough
detail about her — too many gaps.'

'The home she was brought up in
didn't paint much of a picture,' Silas
replied. 'She was apparently quite a

nervous child, but she didn't cause them any real problems. As for her parents — both dead — not that there had been any contact between them and Janice for years.'

'So which way do we turn now?' John Skinner asked, looking to his seniors for inspiration and instruction.

'We turn to the people who knew her,' Silas answered wearily.

'Again?'

'Yes, Skinner, again. We talk to them all again. It's just possible that, this time, someone will say the very thing we want to hear. Someone will give us the link — it's got to be there somewhere.'

'So, who do we start with, sir?'

'Well,' Silas pondered, 'the landlord has known her longer than most, let's have another word with him, shall we?'

★ ★ ★

'I know we've talked to you before, Mr. Allsworth,' Silas began in rueful tone, 'but we do need as much detail about Janice Perry's life as we can get.'

246

'Yes, well my daughter's minding the shop at the moment, but if she gets busy I'll have to pop down and help her out.'

'Understood. We'll try not to keep you long.'

'I'll have to set about letting this place again,' the grocer said, looking around the flat. 'That's when you chaps have finished poking around up here.'

Silas did not reply, but instead pressed on with the matter in hand.

'Is there anything you've omitted to tell us about Janice Perry, Mr. Allsworth?' he asked. 'It could be something that you feel to be unimportant — not worth a mention — but it may just give us the lead we want.'

'I can't think of anything that I haven't already told you, Chief Inspector Blaire. She wasn't a person that you could get to know very well.'

'Tell us about her character,' Geoff Dixon put in. 'In your first interview, I read that you considered her to be rather common. What made you come to that conclusion?'

'Well, her clothes and makeup . . . and

the way she spoke too. You can tell when a girl's common, can't you? It's just something you can see. I didn't judge the girl, or hold all that against her — I mean she'd had a rough start in life — being in a home and everything. And, give her her due, I always got the rent — even if it was a day or two late — I always got it.'

'Did she bring boyfriends — men friends — up here, Mr. Allsworth?'

The psychologist continued to lead the questioning, with the obvious approval of Silas Blaire and his sergeant.

'Sometimes, I think. I can't tell you much about that because once the shop's shut and cleared up, I'm off home, I don't hang around here in the evenings.'

'No, of course not. And you never saw any men leaving in the morning, when you arrived to open the shop?'

'Not often — now and then.'

'No one, special man, though?'

'No.'

'Would you describe Janice Perry as a nervous person?'

'Nervous? She was a bit jumpy, I suppose — neurotic looking — but

248

perhaps that was because she was always sucking on a cigarette; it makes you look nervy, doesn't it?'

'Would you say that she was sensitive about things — about people?'

'No — no, she wasn't sensitive. In fact, I'd describe her as hard. You couldn't blame the girl, though. Having no family, and being brought up as she was, I should think it would make anybody tough — well, you'd have to be tough to cope on your own in this world, wouldn't you? No, nothing much seemed to get to Janice . . . even when her little boy died, she was upset for a week or two, but she was soon back to normal.'

'Little boy?' Silas echoed the words, while glancing at his colleagues to make certain they were sharing his astonishment. They were.

'Janice Perry had a son?' Geoff Dixon said, taking a slow, deliberate step towards the grocer, as though about to attack him.

'Well, yes,' Mr. Allsworth replied somewhat sheepishly, looking from policeman to psychologist and back again. 'Didn't you know?'

'No,' answered Silas, 'we didn't know.'

'Mm. He died about — ooh — three or four years back, it must have been.'

'Did the child live here in the flat with her, Mr. Allsworth?'

'No, Chief Inspector. He was in a home of some sort — locally. I don't know much about the little lad; I never saw him. He wasn't quite the ticket, I don't think . . . well, he can't have been, can he? Dying so young like that.'

'Do you remember his Christian name?'

'No — no, I don't.'

'Was his surname Perry — or did he take his father's name?'

'Oh, he'd have been called Perry, I think. I don't know the father's name. Janice never spoke about him. Whoever he was, he didn't hang around for long.'

'Thank you, Mr. Allsworth . . . and if you think of anything else . . . anything at all . . . '

'Yes, Chief inspector, I'll get in touch.'

Geoff Dixon drove Silas back to the incident room, while John Skinner went, in the police car, to check the date on which the death of Janice Perry's son had been registered.

'Well, they both had sons, Silas,' Geoff Dixon said triumphantly.

'So have millions of other women — why these two? Surely that isn't the link between them.'

'It's a start.'

'But Benjamin Coles is alive and the Perry boy is dead.'

'Mm. We have to find out everything we can about these children. It would be very useful if we could locate the father of Janice Perry's son.'

'Yes, I agree with you there.'

'What are we missing, Silas? I'll bet it's staring us in the face and we're too damned stupid to see it.'

'You speak for yourself, Dixon, there's nothing staring us in the face with these crimes. This lunatic's mind might make some sort of sense to you, but it's all far too obscure for me to understand.'

'Two little boys.' Geoff Dixon was not listening to his friend. 'Two little boys,' he repeated.

'Joanna Coles had a daughter too.'

'I doubt if the little girl had anything to do with the killer's motive.'

'You think it was a sexual thing? Not towards the women — we know there was no sexual assault — but because they were the mothers of sons?' Silas sounded incredulous. 'I've never heard of that one before . . . I mean why?'

'Two little boys,' Geoff Dixon repeated, as though in a trance.

'What on earth could the killer have had against two small children?' This time Silas did not expect an answer, but he got one.

'Nothing — he had nothing against the boys at all — it was their mothers he murdered, Silas.'

★　★　★

When John Skinner entered the incident room, he found Silas and Geoff drinking tea in silence.

'Have you two had a fight?' he asked in jovial earnest.

'No — not yet,' Silas replied. 'Well, when did the Perry boy die?'

'He didn't,' the sergeant said, showing understandable harassment at the negative result of his search, 'at least, not in Hampshire, and not in the last six years.'

'Are you sure? Perhaps you missed something.'

'No, sir. We went right through the registry of deaths in this area, and then checked the whole of the county.'

'That is odd,' Silas shook his head.

'So,' John Skinner went on wearily, 'do we check further afield? The little boy's death must have been registered in another county. Perhaps he was on holiday when he died.'

'Yes, I suppose we'll have . . . '

'No!' Geoff Dixon interrupted emphatically, and with the kind of authority which defied argument. 'We don't have to find out when the child died — because he isn't dead.'

The two policemen stared at the psychologist in wonder, and, after a moment Silas Blaire spoke:

'But Janice Perry told her landlord that her son was dead.'

'Yes, but he isn't dead.'

Now the two policemen stared at each other, more with bewilderment than wonder.

'That flat,' Geoff Dixon murmured, 'what was missing in that awful little flat? I'll tell you, shall I? We went through Janice Perry's personal effects — including her handbag — and we went through everything in her flat, and there was nothing to tell us that she had had a child — not one snapshot — not one toy — nothing.'

'No, but surely, if he was dead . . . ' Silas began apprehensively.

'If she had lost her small son, she would have kept something — a keepsake — a photograph — something. No . . . Janice Perry was not a mother who mourned her child, she was a mother who was trying desperately to forget that he existed. And the best way to stop other people reminding her of his existence was to . . . ?'

'To tell everyone that he was dead,'

Silas uttered, still mystified.

'Exactly. Don't take my word for it, though, make some phone calls,'

'But surely, Geoff, if you're right about this, it only separates Janice Perry even further from Joanna Coles, who doted on her son.'

'Yes, Silas, but why was Janice so determined to eliminate the boy from her life?'

'Single parent — no money — couldn't cope.'

'Not usually reasons for putting your child in a residential home, Silas, and then telling everyone that he's dead. Do you remember what Mr. Allsworth said? What was it? The little lad wasn't quite the ticket. What did he mean by that, I wonder.'

'Well, that he was a sickly child — often unwell. Or retarded maybe — needed extra help at school.'

'Or disabled, Silas, handicapped — like Ben Coles.'

'Disabled and still alive.'

'Yes, I think we've found our link, don't you?'

'Oh I hope so, Geoff — I really do.' Silas turned to John Skinner. 'Right,' he said with renewed confidence and vigour, 'all residential homes in the area — get straight on the phone — find the little Perry boy.'

'Right, sir.'

'He can't be at Darley Hill,' Silas explained to Geoff, 'where Ben Coles goes to school; they don't have boarders there.'

Just two telephone calls later, John Skinner announced that a boy called Andrew Perry was a resident at the Forest Home for handicapped children. He explained that, though the secretary had been reluctant to discuss the matter, she seemed fairly certain that the child was the son of the murdered woman.

Next, Silas Blaire telephoned Darley Hill Special School, not expecting to find anyone still there, it being early evening by now.

'That's a bit of luck,' he said to his colleagues, as he made for the door, 'the headmistress is working late — we'll go to Darley Hill first and then on to the Forest

Home. Are you with us, Geoff?'

'Absolutely!' The plump psychologist was quite breathless with anticipation. He was sure that they were closing in on the murderer, and did not intend to miss a minute of the chase.

It was getting colder, and the strengthening wind rocked the police car as it travelled, at some speed, towards Darley Hill.

'What possible grudge could he have against the mothers of two handicapped boys?' John Skinner wondered aloud. 'I mean, most of us feel pity for the parents of children like that . . . why would he murder them?'

'It's all perfectly reasonable to him,' Geoff Dixon answered, almost dismissively.

'It isn't as though they had similar attitudes towards their sons,' the sergeant continued, 'Joanna Coles wouldn't let her son live in a residential home and she spent every minute she could with him, whereas Janice Perry told everyone that Andrew was dead, and clearly didn't aspire to the title of model mother.'

'No,' Geoff Dixon agreed, 'he wasn't punishing the women for the treatment of these boys.'

'What then?' John Skinner demanded.

'I think he was punishing them for giving life to disabled children. Possibly, he is taking revenge on behalf of the little boys.'

'What a madman,' Silas put in.

'I don't know about that,' Geoff argued, 'it's a very interesting case. You see, he appears to be murdering these women for a reason which makes absolute sense to him, and he enjoys the actual act of killing. Now, this suggests that he is a psychopath and such people are not clinically insane.'

'Really?'

'No. If he is a psychopath, he has a chronic personality disorder, but his brain is functioning normally. Now, if, on the other hand, he feels that he has a mission — maybe he hears voices telling him what he must do to put the world right — then he is mentally ill. With this chap . . . I really don't know . . . I get the feeling that there's a bit of both in him. He feels personal satisfaction when he kills, as though he is driven by his own needs, yet I'm sure he's trying to tell us something at the same time . . . it's fascinating. I'd like to talk to him; I'd like that very much.'

'Well, here's hoping you can, Geoff, and pretty soon too. By the way, I still think he's mad.'

'You use your words, Silas, and I'll use mine.'

'Ah — words — yes!' Silas picked up his phone. 'I'd like a few words with a certain pathologist,' he said, punching out the digits with much annoyance. 'Hello, Simon — Silas Blaire here. I wish I could say that I'm sorry to trouble you at home, but I'm not.'

'What's up now?' the deep voice on the other end of the phone asked, as though he heard nothing but troublesome complaints.

'Janice Perry.' Silas spoke curtly, and John Skinner feared that Blaire the bull was about to surface again.

'What about her?'

'What about her, Simon? The girl had

only had a baby — that's all! I'm sure I would have remembered if you'd mentioned it in your report.'

'Don't be sarcastic, Silas!'

'I'll be as sarcastic as I bloody well like! We should have known! Why didn't you spot it, for Christ's sake?'

'It isn't always detectable.'

'Oh, come on, Simon!'

'No, if the pregnancy was a few years ago, and the baby was very small at birth — premature or just underweight — no stitches and so forth — we can't always pick up on it.'

'Mm. Or perhaps we had one too many at lunchtime.'

'Just what are you suggesting, Silas?'

'I'm suggesting that you should have been able to tell us that Janice Perry had had a child!'

'Medical man now, are you? I'm telling you that it isn't always possible to detect that a woman has given birth — not in certain circumstances. Why don't you check with the hospital records?'

'Don't worry — I intend to! When I've got time, that is.'

'Right. Goodbye then, Silas. Don't work too hard, will you?'

'Happy retirement!' the Chief Inspector called, as the line went dead. 'Useless prat! It's a damned good job he doesn't minister to the living any more. I suppose he can't do too much harm to the deceased.'

★   ★   ★

'As I explained on the telephone, Chief Inspector Blaire,' the headmistress of Darley Hill Special School said, after showing the three men into her office, 'once, I would have said that you were very fortunate to catch me here at this time of day. There's so much paperwork attached to my job now, though, that I find myself spending more and more of my time in this office. I could do with half a dozen secretaries and a fully qualified accountant on hand, I truly could.'

The middle-aged woman, with her wavy grey hair cropped short and her tall, slim body clad in a tailored suit, reminded Silas of the stereotypical headmistress who invariably appeared in the children's detective stories he had read as a boy. She looked at him through thick, ugly spectacles, and awaited his questions with a patience so well cultivated that it was almost tangible.

'I'm afraid it's about the Joanna Coles murder again, Miss Twyford,' Silas began.

'Yes, I thought it probably was,' she replied, her words coming slowly and precisely.

'There has been another, similar murder in the district.'

'Yes, I read about it . . . quite dreadful.'

'Well, Miss Twyford, we believe that we've found a link between Joanna Coles and Janice Perry — the second woman to be murdered.'

'Have you?'

'Yes, they both had disabled children — sons.'

'Good grief. The other poor woman's boy doesn't attend this school though, I'm sure.'

'No, no, Andrew Perry is at the Forest Home.'

'Oh yes, I see. He's a resident there, I suppose.'

'That's right. Now, Miss Twyford, it's very likely that our killer has visited both this school and the Forest Home — that's where he met, or at least saw, the boys and their mothers too.'

'Oh dear, that's really quite horrifying — unnerving — are you sure?'

'It is the most probable solution to the problem of how he found these two women, I'm afraid.'

'Well, how can I help you, Chief Inspector Blaire?'

'We need to know the names of people — visitors — who come to both schools for some reason. In the case of Joanna Coles, we are fairly certain that she knew her murderer, so it would be someone who was quite well known to the parents.'

'I can't speak for the Forest Home, of course, but I can tell you the visitors who come here — regular visitors anyway.'

'That would be very helpful, Miss Twyford. We'll be going to the Forest Home later and we can compare lists then.'

'Do you want the names of professional people — like the school dentist?'

'Yes. Absolutely everyone you can think of.'

'Right, well, here are the names of the school's doctor, dentist and the two nurses who visit periodically.'

The efficient woman took a piece of paper from a large filing cabinet and passed it to Silas.

'Thank you, Miss Twyford — anyone else?'

'Oh, yes, Chief Inspector, we do have quite a few visitors, and they're not all as easy to name as the medical personnel, but I'll do my best. Now, let's see, we have a musical group, who come to entertain the children about once a month. Handicapped children get a great deal of pleasure from music, you know, Chief Inspector. It's very therapeutic for them too.'

'Yes, I'm sure,' Silas said, trying to curtail what looked like turning into a long explanation of the school's policy on entertainment.

Miss Twyford delved into a different drawer of the filing cabinet.

'Yes, here we are,' she announced

triumphantly, 'this is the name and number of the group's leader anyway. But they're such lovely young people, I really can't believe that they'd do anything so ghastly. They visit old people's homes in the area too . . . they're quite splendid.'

'Well, we'll see, Miss Twyford. We have to check out all possibilities.'

'Yes, I suppose you do. Now — who else is there?' She stood still, as though caught in a time warp, while considering who else the Chief Inspector needed to know about. 'There's the travelling puppet theatre, of course,' she exclaimed, pointing her index finger at nothing in particular and attacking the filing cabinet once more. 'Yes, that's them.' Another piece of paper was thrust at Silas Blaire. 'They've been coming here for years; I really can't believe it's one of them.'

'I'm sure that, when we find our murderer, Miss Twyford,' Silas said quietly, 'there will be a great many people who won't be able to believe that he's committed these awful crimes.'

'Yes, I suppose that's the way these

things work out,' she replied dreamily, 'quite a gruesome thought that, isn't it?'

'Any more visitors?'

'Er — yes — Alex Dunbar brings ponies quite often, so that the children can have rides. She's kindness itself — she really is. One of her sons usually comes with her. They're a very wealthy family.'

'Yes — the big stud farm and stables out of town — near Darley Village — that's theirs, isn't it?'

'That's right.'

'Anyone else, Miss Twyford?'

'I can't think of anybody just at the moment, Chief Inspector Blaire, though I'm sure there must be others. I'll ask the staff tomorrow — then I'll phone you with any more names and addresses we can think of — how's that?'

'That'll be great. Thank you for your help, Miss Twyford.'

Silas made for the door.

'I'd like to ask something,' Geoff Dixon said, breaking what for him was a remarkably long silence. 'Could you tell me, Miss Twyford, whether or not any of these visitors are themselves disabled?'

'Er — no — no.' She paused for a moment to double-check her thoughts. 'No none of them are disabled.'

★ ★ ★

By the time they had fought against the gale force wind, which battered them on their way from school building to car, the policemen and Geoff Dixon felt as though they had taken part in a short, but vigorous brawl.

'You think that he could be handicapped in some way?' John Skinner panted, as the car doors were quickly shut against the weather.

'It would make a lot more sense if he were,' Geoff Dixon replied, 'but he can't be in a wheelchair, can he? He'd never have been able to commit the crimes.'

'Absolutely,' Silas agreed adamantly. 'He must be able-bodied — the angle of the knife wounds showed him to be fairly tall too.'

'Yes, I remember reading that in the reports,' Geoff said thoughtfully. 'It would make it so much easier to explain his actions, though, if he were disabled. I can't get into this chap's head . . . there's too much that I don't understand about him.'

The three occupants of the police car sunk into what would have been a pensive silence, but for the throb of the engine and the thundering wind outside.

'This poor little soul hasn't got much left, has he?' Silas Blaire spoke suddenly and left his two colleagues somewhat confused. 'The little lad at the Forest Home — Andrew Perry,' he elucidated.

'Mm . . . mm,' came the general consensus, and then:

'How's your son, Silas?' Geoff Dixon inquired cheerily, 'James, isn't it?'

'He's very well, Geoff, thank you.' Silas was unsure whether or not to confide in his friends about the feelings he had been trying to ignore for the past day or so. 'To tell you the truth,' he went on, deciding that it might help to talk about things, 'he came to see me earlier this week. He's off on holiday with his grandfather — and his mother — the

Seychelles, I believe he said.'

'Very nice too,' John Skinner put in, almost drooling at the thought of such affluence.

'Mm, I suppose so.' Silas was obviously unimpressed. 'Helen — my wife — has got a new boyfriend. Not that James said much about him, but he's apparently going on holiday with them . . . good luck to him.'

'You wish that James hadn't come to see you, don't you, Silas?' Geoff asked, his understanding of the human mind being evident from his kindly words.

'He stayed for a couple of hours,' Silas continued, either choosing not to answer Geoff Dixon, or not really hearing his question. 'I don't know why — once he'd told me about their forthcoming holiday, we didn't know what to say to each other. It was as though we were strangers. I sat there trying to think of something to talk about — something we had in common — and the worst part of it was that I knew he was doing exactly the same thing. We briefly touched on my work, and on the good health of his mother and grandpa, but it could all have been said in five minutes. Do you know, Geoff, I was relieved when he left . . . my own son, and I couldn't wait for him to go. I've lost him completely now . . . I know that. At one time, I thought that he might reject my father's overpowering and possessive ways, just as I did, but not now . . . no, he'll never come back to me now.'

'Here we are, sir,' John Skinner announced, relieved to be able to change the mood, 'The Forest Home for Handicapped Children'

It was between eight o'clock and eight thirty when the matron of the home showed the three men into her office.

'This is a fairly quiet time of day to visit us,' the comely woman explained, ' most of the children are settled down for the night, and the staff have a little time for themselves.'

'We've come about Andrew Perry,' Silas said, wasting no time.

'Yes, that's no surprise.' The matron's smile was quite charming and her manner effervescent.

'You didn't feel it necessary to contact

270

the police, when you saw in the newspapers that Andrew's mother was a murder victim?' Silas was direct, but quietly so.

'It wasn't necessary to contact you, Chief Inspector, his mother's death will make very little difference to Andrew, and there was nothing at all that I could have told you to help with your investigations.'

'You should have let me be the judge of that,' Silas replied.

'Perhaps I should, but I knew you'd come to us if you thought we could help. Isn't it usual for you to be the pursuers, rather than the pursued?'

Silas grinned.

'Andrew will stay here then?' he asked, his tone lightening.

'Yes. When a child is admitted to the Forest Home, the parent or guardian signs a declaration stating what they wish to happen to their child in the event of their own death. As you can imagine, this makes life a lot simpler for everyone — not that many of our parents die that young, of course. Sometimes, there are requests for children to be moved to different parts of the country — to be near grandparents or whatever. But in Andrew's case there were no such instructions. Miss Perry, being Andrew's only known relative, wished him to stay here, with his friends and carers that he is familiar with. He is now completely in the care of the county, and has the status of an orphan.'

'Poor little chap,' Silas murmured.

'Yes, when you're seven years old and severely handicapped, you can do with someone of your own, but there we are, Andrew Perry has no one now — not much of a start in life, is it?'

Silas glanced at his two colleagues and then faced the matron with eager, earnest eyes.

'Would it be all right if I visited him from time to time?' he asked cautiously. 'I know I can't be like a real relative to the boy, but he'd get to know me, wouldn't he? I could bring him toys some-times . . . '

'I think that that would be a very good idea, Chief Inspector Blaire,' the matron replied. 'And I know that Andrew would look forward to your visits; he's a very friendly little boy.'

'Good, I'll do that then.' Silas nodded with satisfaction. 'Did his mother visit him very often?' he went on.

'No.' The matron bowed her head, as though she was remorseful on behalf of the murdered woman. 'She came to see Andrew only once a year, I'm afraid.'

'Once?'

'Yes, Chief Inspector, your visits will, no doubt, be more frequent than Miss Perry's were.'

'Just once a year?' Silas repeated.

'Yes, she visited Andrew every year on his birthday — that was all.'

'Did she visit him recently then? When is his birthday?'

Silas looked excitedly at his sergeant and Geoff Dixon; this could be the bit of luck they had been waiting for.

'Hang on — I'll check. I'm sure it wasn't that long ago — her last visit. No — here we are — Andrew Perry — date of birth — February the twentieth.'

'Right, now, Matron, can you tell us of

any visitors who came here on that particular day?'

'The same day as Miss Perry's visit? Andrew's birthday?'

'Yes. We believe that the murderer is someone who singled out his victims on visits to this home and Darley Hill Special School, where Joanna Coles's son is a pupil.'

'I see. Well, let me look in the main diary — that's the best place to find out if anyone was visiting.'

'Thanks.'

Silas grinned as Geoff Dixon held up crossed fingers on both hands.

'Er . . . February the twentieth — yes — the Dunbars visited the school that day. They brought their ponies so that the children could have rides. It was all a great success.'

'The Dunbars!' Silas exclaimed. 'Thank you — thank you very much! Now, who came exactly? Which members of the family?'

His voice carried urgency and his eyes a certain relief.

'Well, Mrs. Dunbar came, and her son

— the elder of the two, so she was telling me — er — Guy — that's his name. But, just a minute, Chief Inspector Blaire.' The matron raised her hand in protest. 'I know you can't go by appearances, but the Dunbars really are the most charming people. I'm sure they could have had nothing to do with these dreadful murders. It's ridiculous to think that they could have been involved. I mean, why would they? All their work with the children is voluntary — they make absolutely nothing out of it. I remember saying to my deputy, after their visit, that it's a shame there aren't more people like them in the world . . . caring, unselfish people. I had quite a long talk to Mrs. Dunbar, and she really wants to give our children pleasure — that's the only reason she visits homes and schools like this one. And as for her son, well, he's an absolute marvel. Giving up his free time to come and help his mother — and him with his own handicap to cope with. Some young men would just sit at home and . . . '

'Just a minute,' Silas interrupted, 'did you say that Guy Dunbar has a handicap?'

'Well, yes. He's a haemophiliac — his mother was telling me. His condition is deteriorating quite rapidly now — poor thing.'

Geoff Dixon stared at Silas with subdued jubilation.

'That's our man,' he said softly, 'that's our man.'

The matron stood alone in her office, her three guests having departed swiftly, and with only the briefest of goodbyes.

18

Guy and Alex sat in the drawing room of Dunbar House enjoying an after dinner brandy. It would be the last such evening they would ever share, a thought which afforded Guy much pleasure.

He would allow himself no doubts and tolerate no grief . . . he would never know remorse.

'I hope it wasn't this windy when your father crossed the water to Ireland,' Alex reflected, 'he's never been a particularly good sailor.'

'He'll be all right — they docked hours ago, didn't they?'

'Hopefully. I do miss him when he's away.'

Guy wondered whether his father and Aunt Kate would get together after his mother's death. That would be very gratifying.

'I think I'll get an early night,' Guy

said, stretching his arms above his head and yawning.

'Yes, I won't be long myself. It isn't the sort of night to sit up late, is it? I'll bet there'll be a few fences down in the morning.'

'I guess so.'

'I hope Toby and Tess don't lose too many tiles off their cottage. Toby was saying, only yesterday, that they'd got some dodgy ones. The place needs a complete new roof, I think.'

Guy had no intention of entering into a long conversation with his mother about Toby and Tess and their cottage, which was currently one of her favourite topics.

'Well, I'm off, Mother,' he announced, hobbling towards the drawing room door.

'All right, darling. I'll be in soon to do your injection — I'll just finish my drink.'

★ ★ ★

'One thing we can be fairly certain of,' John Skinner began, as he drove the police car out of Darley New Town and towards Dunbar House, 'if Guy Dunbar has any sense at all, he'll be safely at home tonight, and not out and about intending to murder again.'

'True,' Silas agreed, 'but the sooner we talk to him and get him back to the station, the happier I'll be.'

'Absolutely,' Geoff Dixon put in decisively.

'What about proof, though, sir?' Sergeant Skinner asked, pitching his voice above the noise of the howling gales which struck at the car. 'Isn't the evidence a bit thin on the ground?'

'Yes, it is, but when we question him — who knows what he'll tell us, especially when Geoff gets his turn, eh, Geoff?'

'I should say so!' the psychologist answered resolutely.

The wind was so strong by now that the trees, which edged the narrow lane up to Dunbar House, swayed in the beam of the car's headlights, their branches shaking like a thousand angry arms.

'You're as certain as you can be that Guy Dunbar is the killer, aren't you, Geoff?' Silas asked, feeling the need to check that most important of facts.

'I'd lay money on it,' the psychologist answered, grinning broadly, 'and I don't part with the pennies lightly.'

'No, I know that, Geoff, I've been in the pub with you more than once.'

★   ★   ★

Guy lay in his bed, awaiting his mother's arrival. This would be positively the last injection of factor eight that she would ever give him and the joy which this brought to his heart, was immense. He did not know who would inject him in the future and he did not care. It would not be her, with her cheerful and inane witterings. It would not be her.

A smile lifted Guy's countenance as he contemplated Alex taking her final shower, and then getting into bed for the last, brief, living sleep before her death.

He stared at the heavy, brass paper-weight, which stood on a small desk near to his bed, and imagined what the sound would be like as it met her temple, and cracked open that most fragile part of her skull. He wondered if her eyes would open momentarily . . . if she would see him . . . and know.

★   ★   ★

'What the . . . ?' John Skinner stopped the car sharply, causing his two passengers to sit up smartly in their seats, and be thankful for safety belts.

'What is it?' Silas barked.

'Just what we need, sir. The wind's brought a tree down right across the lane.'

'Oh hell!'

'Shall I phone through for assistance, sir?'

'Let's have a look first, Skinner. Is it a monster of a tree, or could the three of us move it?'

Silas and his sergeant fought their way to the front of the car and inspected the cause of the hold up. The deserted lane was lit only by the car's headlights, but they could see the tree lying across their path, and assess its size and weight.

'I think we could move it, sir,' Skinner yelled, his voice almost lost in the wind. 'There's some rope in the boot; I'm sure the car would pull it away.'

'Yes, let's have a go. I want to get home tonight, and if we wait for assistance we could be here for hours.'

Silas pointed to the car, and the two policemen returned to the shelter of its interior, in order to acquaint Geoff Dixon with their immediate plans.

'We're going to tie a rope round the tree and pull it away with the car,' John Skinner explained to the intrigued psychologist.

'Oh good!' he exclaimed with some relief, 'I'm glad you don't need the use of my muscle power, because there isn't much of it.'

'You can reverse the car, Geoff,' Silas suggested, 'when Skinner and I have got the rope secure, all right?'

'Good idea,' came the keen reply, 'ready when you are.'

Geoff Dixon settled himself in the driver's seat, while the two policemen ventured out again to tie the rope round the wayward tree.

★   ★   ★

'Right, darling,' Alex said, as she set out the equipment needed for Guy's injection in her usual efficient way, 'here we are then.'

Guy stared at the ceiling. After all these years, he still preferred to avert his eyes as the syringe was made ready to pierce his skin.

'Poor you,' he whispered lovingly.

'Why poor me?' Alex asked, somewhat bemused, as she continued with the preparations.

'It must be a drag having to inject me all the time. You must hate the sight of syringes as much as I do.'

'That doesn't enter my head, darling. It has to be done — so I do it — no problem. Do you know, I remember Toby crying once — I suppose he must have been about four years old — he went on for ages. Eventually he told your father and I that he was crying because he wanted to have injections too. He was jealous of the extra attention you got . . . children! They're full of surprises.'

'Stupid bugger,' Guy chuckled.

'Oh, he was little more than a baby,

Guy; I'm sure that the novelty would soon have worn off.'

'Too damned right it would!'

She had cleaned the skin and the syringe was ready. Guy was about to receive the last dose of factor eight that his mother would ever administer to him.

Alex gave her son his injection.

'How's that, darling?' she murmured.

'Fine — didn't feel a thing,' he joked as usual, except that this time euphoria washed over his mind like a soothing balm.

'Good.' She kissed his forehead tenderly. 'Sleep well, Guy,' she said. 'Goodnight — God bless.'

When she reached the door of Guy's room, Alex turned, and mother and son smiled at each other for the very last time.

In that second, in that smile, a lifetime's love passed between them.

★   ★   ★

'Right, the rope's secure!' Silas bellowed through the foul night to Geoff Dixon. 'Now, gently reverse until I raise my hand. Go to the left, then John and I should be able to push it the rest of the way into the side of the lane!'

'Right — ready!' Geoff replied, signalling frantically.

The engine of the police car laboured to drag the small tree from its obstructive position. John Skinner and Silas Blaire, their clothes flapping violently about them, propelled the young silver birch, with as much force as they could summon, to the edge of the road. The rope was quickly untied, and the policemen rejoined their colleague in the car.

'Only about a mile now,' Silas sighed, as he recovered his breath, 'off we go, Geoff. You can take us the rest of the way.'

'I had a date tonight,' John Skinner said wistfully.

'She'll understand,' Silas reassured.

'Yes,' Geoff Dixon added, 'I should think she'd be favourably impressed when she finds out that you've been in pursuit of a murderer.'

'I think she'd be more favourably impressed,' the sergeant moaned, 'if I turned up for a date on time.'

'Here we are,' Silas announced, 'Dunbar House. Now let's go and talk to Mr. Guy Dunbar.'

★   ★   ★

As the Chief Inspector fought his way up the steps which fell gracefully away from the main entrance of the mansion, he forgot briefly about the gales which tugged at his clothes, and made the world such a turbulent place. He forgot about the two colleagues by his side. He even forgot about Guy Dunbar and the murdered women.

Just for a moment, the splendour of the house filled his mind with thoughts of his own youth, which had been spent in a vast mansion such as this. When he remembered his old home, however, it was not its spacious elegance which he called to mind, nor the opulence which emanated from every antique that furnished its interior. It was discord and loneliness that returned to sting Silas Blaire's heart when he thought of his early years.

Silas eschewed his memories. He had no wish to remain in the past. Nostalgia held no joys for him.

'All right, sir?' Sergeant Skinner shouted, as they awaited a reply from within.

'Yes — yes, I'm fine. Full of thoughts, that's all.'

The door to Dunbar House, and the evening's events, opened slowly.

19

'I had to end my son's life, Chief Inspector,' Alex Dunbar said serenely, as she sipped a large whisky in the drawing room of her home. 'From the moment the doctors told me how his condition would eventually deteriorate, I knew that, when he had suffered enough, I would understand, and I would end his misery.'

'You gave him an overdose of his usual drugs, Mrs. Dunbar?' Silas asked gently.

'Yes. It was a mixture of the various drugs he had been prescribed — in huge amounts. It all went in the syringe. He just lay there, as usual, while I injected him. He trusted me implicitly. We had a very special relationship — Guy and myself. I know it's what he really wanted . . . I've no doubts about that at all. It was quite uncanny, you know, when I gave him that very last injection . . . just for a second, in his eyes . . . there was a look . . . almost as though he knew that we were sharing our last moments together. But that was just my imagination . . . he had no idea . . . no idea at all.'

'Your doctor is on his way, Mrs. Dunbar. If you'd like him to give you a mild sedative before we go to the police station, that would be all right.'

'No, Chief Inspector Blaire. We've no need for the doctor here, not now that Guy has gone.'

'Your younger son and your husband have both been contacted too. Toby should be here very soon.'

'They will be able to visit me, won't they, Chief Inspector?' Alex asked, doubt clouding her eyes for the first time. 'Phillip and Toby and Tess will be able to visit me, won't they? I couldn't bear it if I didn't see them.'

'Your family will be able to visit you, Mrs. Dunbar, don't worry about that.'

Alex stared straight ahead of her, quite calm again.

I tried to make his life happy,' she said. 'That was always my main aim — to make his life as happy as it could be — and then to end it when the right time came. Over the years, I've become strangely used to the idea . . . I've had a long time to prepare myself for what I had to do tonight. It was right, Chief Inspector, right and just that I should take his life . . . it was me that gave him life after all. I've always protected him from any danger — any harm. Sometimes I used to think that I should let him go — let him have a horse and a car — if he'd had an accident, he might have been killed, and then . . . and then I wouldn't have had to . . . But no, that wasn't the right way. I had to do it. That's what Guy would have wanted.'

'Toby Dunbar has arrived, sir,' John Skinner reported from his vantage-point by the drawing room door.

'Don't let him in for a moment,' Alex pleaded, 'I just want a minute more.'

Silas raised his hand, and the sergeant went to delay Toby in the hall.

Geoff Dixon moved slowly towards Alex, and stood with his hand on her shoulder.

'Is there anything else you want to tell us, Mrs. Dunbar?' he entreated, glancing at Silas with hope in his eyes.

'Yes, there is,' Alex answered coldly. 'In case you aren't aware of the fact, Chief Inspector Blaire, you have no need to search for the murderer of those two young women any longer — it was my son. You see, there was nothing he could keep secret from me. I knew absolutely everything about Guy — absolutely everything. I believe you'll find the weapons, and so forth, at the bottom of a natural well, in the woods near the house. He threw the controls of a very expensive electric train-set down there once, many years ago . . . when he wanted to make it disappear from his life.' She paused. 'You mustn't think badly of Guy, Chief Inspector.' Alex's voice was weaker now. 'He was not an evil person, you know . . . he was confused and tormented, but not evil. Killing those two women . . . that was . . . that was only a part of the man. That was the dark side of Guy Dunbar.'

★ ★ ★

Several police cars stood on the drive of Dunbar House by the time Silas Blaire,

291

his sergeant and Geoff Dixon emerged from its grand front entrance.

The formerly raging wind had diminished substantially, and by now was little more than an over-zealous breeze.

Toby Dunbar had already accompanied his mother to the Darley New Town Police Station, with two young officers and one police woman in attendance.

'If that tree hadn't blown down,' John Skinner began, 'we might have . . . '

'Might have got there before she gave him the lethal injection,' Silas interrupted.

'Well yes, sir.'

'And what then?' Geoff Dixon asked, awaiting no one's reply, and displaying an aura of grave certainty about him. 'Alex Dunbar would have seen her son charged with murder, tried and punished. At least, this way, she knows that she's saved him from all that.'

'What about the victims and their families, though?' Sergeant Skinner argued. 'It isn't really justice, is it?'

'He's dead,' the psychologist answered, 'there must be some justice in that surely.'

'Imagine watching your child grow up and devoting your life to him, like Alex Dunbar did.' Silas said, his eyes staring at the gravel drive on which the three men stood, his voice low and melancholy. 'Watching him develop, watching him learn, and all the time, preparing yourself for the day that you're going to murder him.'

'I think,' John Skinner put in, 'that Guy Dunbar inherited more than haemophilia from his mother. I think she is as mad as he was, in her own way.'

'She didn't murder her son,' Geoff asserted with half a smile. 'In her eyes, she gave him his freedom.'

'Well, I'd like to have seen him do a long stretch behind bars,' John Skinner maintained, looking to Silas for agreement.

The Chief Inspector turned, unblinking, to his young sergeant.

'Some people live the whole of their life behind bars, Skinner,' he reflected, 'in their own private and permanent prison. Come on now, let's go home, shall we? Guy Dunbar will never hurt anyone else. He's gone . . . dark side and all.'

We do hope that you have enjoyed reading this large print book.

Did you know that all of our titles are available for purchase?

We publish a wide range of high quality large print books including:
Romances, Mysteries, Classics
General Fiction
Non Fiction and Westerns

Special interest titles available in large print are:
The Little Oxford Dictionary
Music Book, Song Book
Hymn Book, Service Book

Also available from us courtesy of Oxford University Press:
Young Readers' Dictionary
(large print edition)
Young Readers' Thesaurus
(large print edition)

For further information or a free brochure, please contact us at:
Ulverscroft Large Print Books Ltd.,
The Green, Bradgate Road, Anstey,
Leicester, LE7 7FU, England.
Tel: (00 44) **0116 236 4325**
Fax: (00 44) **0116 234 0205**

Other titles in the
Linford Mystery Library:

THE DARK BUREAU

Ernest Dudley

The newspaper headlines screamed, 'Ace Television Personality Vanishes' . . . Following transmission of his programme *Meet Your Criminals*, an exposé of a big crime organisation operating in London, Tod Archer disappears — possibly due to amnesia. But Algy Dark, chief of the Dark Bureau, knows better: Archer is one of his men and the Bureau has been too efficient against crime. And Dark knows that whoever has removed Archer is also the power behind the crime-gangs, a man known mysteriously as — 'The Butterfly' . . .

BLACK MARIA, M.A.

John Russell Fearn

When Ralph Black, chain store magnate, was found shot by his own gun in his locked library, the New York police pronounced it as suicide. However, family members believe it was murder. His sister in England, Maria Black, M.A., Headmistress of a girls' school, wants to discover the truth. She travels to America, and with her penchant for solving crimes, sets to work to trace the mysterious plot against her brother to the final unmasking of the amazing truth.

FOOTSTEPS OF ANGELS

E. C. Tubb

Empire builder Max Feyman had ruthlessly gained control of an invention called the 'zipdrive', a system of ultra-fast space travel. But his world is shattered when his daughter Celia, holidaying on the moon, is suddenly rendered unable to walk or speak — dependent on others to remain alive. Then, across the solar system, others are also struck down. Feyman must find a cure for the mysterious affliction that threatens not only the life of his only daughter — but also humanity itself!

THE CROOKED INN

Ernest Dudley

Max Mitchell and Dan Evans, two London playwrights, are seeking atmosphere and characters for a play. But when they travel to Wales for inspiration they find more than they bargained for. They arrive in Llanberis on a stormy night, and are forced to stay at the wrong hotel, The Crooked Inn. Then, as they face some disparate characters, and The Crooked Inn's connections to the gaol-break of a murderer, they become involved in a real-life drama of murder and mystery.